‖‖‖‖‖‖‖‖‖‖‖‖‖‖‖‖‖‖‖‖‖‖‖‖‖

✓ **W9-AJS-836**

"I know you miss Mom, honey. You realize you can always ask me about her, right?"

"Of course I do, Dad. But you have to admit you weren't as close to Mom as Claire was, not when you were little or even my age."

Dutch looked into eyes as brown as Natalie's had been. When did this little button of a girl turn into a young woman?

"No. You're right about that." Claire had been a part of Natalie's life forever.

Dutch kissed Sasha's forehead. "You can go to Claire's farm with me next time, but promise me you won't get your hopes up too much."

"Dad, I'm not going to force you guys to be friends or anything. I get it." Her posture of maturity almost fooled him.

He knew Sasha didn't really get it. Sasha didn't want him to think she was playing matchmaker, but he saw the warning signs. She had no idea that once upon a time, he and Claire hadn't needed a matchmaker....

Dear Reader,

Claire and Dutch's story is one I've wanted to write for a while. So many people talk about their high school sweethearts, whom they still remember, still think of. I wanted to explore this concept, but from a different angle—Claire and Dutch each allowed the other to get away all those years ago. But not before they inflicted emotional damage on themselves and those around them.

Atoning for past mistakes and hurts is one of the hardest things we ever have to do. First we need to admit that we messed up, then we have to mend fences with the people we've hurt. Claire thinks she only has to make amends to her deceased best friend, Natalie, via her relationship with Natalie's daughter, Sasha. But Claire learns that the first person she needs to make amends to is herself.

I enjoyed digging through Claire and Dutch's emotional history and bringing the love they share today to life. I hope you find their story as mesmerizing to read as I did to write.

I use whatever places our Navy lifestyle takes us as my settings. In this book I enjoyed writing about the fictional town of Dovetail, Maryland. Our time in nearby Annapolis was great and we left with new friends, not something that happens every tour.

Keep reading and remember to cherish your friends—today.

Peace,

Geri Krotow

Sasha's Dad
Geri Krotow

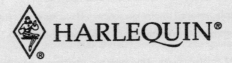

TORONTO • NEW YORK • LONDON
AMSTERDAM • PARIS • SYDNEY • HAMBURG
STOCKHOLM • ATHENS • TOKYO • MILAN • MADRID
PRAGUE • WARSAW • BUDAPEST • AUCKLAND

If you purchased this book without a cover you should be aware
that this book is stolen property. It was reported as "unsold and
destroyed" to the publisher, and neither the author nor the
publisher has received any payment for this "stripped book."

Recycling programs
for this product may
not exist in your area.

ISBN-13: 978-0-373-71642-5

SASHA'S DAD

Copyright © 2010 by Geri Krotow.

All rights reserved. Except for use in any review, the reproduction or
utilization of this work in whole or in part in any form by any electronic,
mechanical or other means, now known or hereafter invented, including
xerography, photocopying and recording, or in any information storage
or retrieval system, is forbidden without the written permission of the
publisher, Harlequin Enterprises Limited, 225 Duncan Mill Road,
Don Mills, Ontario, Canada M3B 3K9.

This is a work of fiction. Names, characters, places and incidents are
either the product of the author's imagination or are used fictitiously,
and any resemblance to actual persons, living or dead, business
establishments, events or locales is entirely coincidental.

This edition published by arrangement with Harlequin Books S.A.

For questions and comments about the quality of this book
please contact us at Customer_eCare@Harlequin.ca.

® and TM are trademarks of the publisher. Trademarks indicated with
® are registered in the United States Patent and Trademark Office, the
Canadian Trade Marks Office and in other countries.

www.eHarlequin.com

Printed in U.S.A.

ABOUT THE AUTHOR

Currently living in Moscow, Russia, former naval intelligence officer and U.S. Naval Academy graduate Geri Krotow writes about the people and places she's been lucky enough to encounter. Geri loves to hear from her readers. You can e-mail her via her Web site and blog, www.gerikrotow.com.

Books by Geri Krotow

HARLEQUIN SUPERROMANCE
1547—WHAT FAMILY MEANS

HARLEQUIN EVERLASTING LOVE
20—A RENDEZVOUS TO REMEMBER

Don't miss any of our special offers. Write to us at the following address for information on our newest releases.

Harlequin Reader Service
U.S.: 3010 Walden Ave., P.O. Box 1325, Buffalo, NY 14269
Canadian: P.O. Box 609, Fort Erie, Ont. L2A 5X3

With love for my dad, Ed.
You were my first hero.

Acknowledgments

With thanks to Mary Sellers at Homestead Gardens in Davidsonville, MD—thanks for the day with the llamas, and all the wonderful information.

Thanks to the Bay Dale Walkers— Debbie, Cyndi and Jenn.

As always thanks to Mary B. and Patti M. for watching my six.

CHAPTER ONE

TEARS OF FEAR and frustration welled in Claire Renquist's eyes as she swiped at her cheeks with her waffle-knit shirtsleeve. She knew there'd be long days and early mornings when she decided to start an agricultural business. But she'd never expected the gut-tugging angst that sideswiped her when one of her animals was in trouble.

Claire's hands shook as she pulled out her cell phone and punched in Dr. Charlie Flynn's speed dial. Her vet and family friend never let her down. When Claire moved back to Dovetail, Maryland, two years ago she'd asked Charlie to doctor her animals. He'd promised to come whenever she called.

She stood outside the modest barn she'd refurbished. Cell phone reception was better out here, away from under the thick oak beams. Although it was pitch-dark and cold for the middle of March, the full moon lit up the surrounding fields and rolling hills.

Claire stared numbly at the view and not for the first time wondered why she'd done it—not only moving back to Dovetail, but starting a llama farm. She'd been a political reporter, assigned to the White House press corps, for heaven's sake. Her TV network had given her free rein and allowed her to follow the president wherever and whenever she wanted. And she'd been able to branch off if a story called for it, visiting some of the most far-flung places on earth. Today she had her pick of consulting jobs where she could name her own salary, which helped her fund the farm until it got on its financial feet—

"Dr. Flynn's answering service. May I help you?"

"Oh, I was expecting Charlie." She caught her breath and forced herself to *think*.

"This is Claire Renquist at Llama Fiber Haven. Can you please tell him I need him immediately? I have a dam in distress with a breech birth." A long mewl came from inside the barn. "Tell him to hurry."

She snapped her phone shut and shoved it into her down vest pocket. Her nerves warred with her training, which allowed her to remain calm in most crises. Charlie was going to be annoyed with her. He'd been adamant that she call him as soon as she suspected Stormy was in labor. But she'd wanted to claim this first birth as her own. The llamas had become part of her life from the moment they'd arrived here in Dovetail. She'd nurtured them, rejoiced when Stormy became pregnant by artificial insemination and at times felt like one with her animals.

She'd been so sure she had everything under control.

Until labor began two weeks earlier than expected. She should have called Charlie as soon as she thought anything was amiss.

But she hadn't.

Stupid. Selfish.

She ignored the critical voice. This wasn't about *her.*

Claire rounded the corner of the stall and looked at her prized female llama. Stormy's pecan-colored coat shook as her ribs heaved from the effort of breathing through her labor pains. Pains that should've been over after Claire helped birth the baby llama who stood blinking up at her, his brown eyes globes of innocence and trust. He mewled at her, shivering. He'd walked away from the heater she'd left him next to.

"Come on, baby." She led the cria closer to the warmth and rushed back to Stormy's side. Llamas weren't usually vocal, and if Stormy had been the one mewling… Claire distracted herself by keeping her focus on calming Stormy.

"You did a wonderful job, momma," she crooned to the three-year-old llama.

But Stormy wasn't done. Claire swallowed down her fear. There was another calf in Stormy's womb; she'd felt the hooves after the first cria was born. Plus the dam's apparent discomfort alarmed her. It wasn't typical for llama's to convey distress during birth.

Twins. Claire groaned.

Twins weren't a cause for joy, not in the llama world. They often meant death for the dam.

"Hang in there, Stormy." Claire rested her hand on Stormy's side, hoping to calm her. It was an impossible task as her own anxiety threatened to shatter her brittle composure.

DANIEL "DUTCH" ARCHER, Jr., squinted against the glare of the bathroom light.

"Humph." He groaned as he splashed cold water on his face.

Waking up from a deep sleep to go out and make a house call wasn't unusual for a large-animal veterinarian. Especially in rural Maryland.

What *was* unusual was his reaction to this message from his service.

Emotions he never wanted to feel again. The one person on earth he never wanted to deal with again, not at such close proximity.

Claire Renquist.

"Damn it." He yanked open his bathroom door and strode back into his bedroom. This was just another call.

Like hell it is.

Underneath the layers of indifference, resentment, anger and a sheer distaste some might even describe as hate, Dutch recognized the tickle of anticipation. And he despised the part of himself that enjoyed it.

It wasn't anxiety over the difficult job to come—saving a cria twin and the dam. It was knowing that in a few short miles he'd come face-to-face with the woman he'd avoided so carefully for the past two years.

He grunted. *Two years, hell; try more than a decade.*

Sure, they'd had unavoidable run-ins around town since Claire moved back to Dovetail, but they'd never spoken a word. The few times their eyes had met they'd looked away, each refusing to acknowledge the other. Like strangers, and that was how Dutch wanted it to stay.

If he'd been more mature when he'd chosen Claire's closest friend, Natalie, over Claire all those years ago, he would never have encouraged Natalie to remain friends with Claire. He and Claire had drifted apart during their senior year in high school. After the horrific accident that had killed Dutch's best friend, Tom, Dutch had gone to comfort Tom's twin sister, Natalie, and, in a moment that changed the rest of all their lives, made love to her.

His relationship with Claire was irrevocably severed.

Never mind their childhood bond. Never mind that Claire had christened him with the name "Dutch" when, at age three, her pronunciation of Daniel Archer had become "Darch" and then "Dutch." Dutch's mother had loved it and so the name stuck.

He pulled on his work jeans and made a mental note to leave a note by his sister, Ginny's, coffee mug. If not for Ginny he couldn't keep making these late-night calls. Hopefully he'd be back before Sasha left for school.

He sighed and yanked a sweatshirt over his head.

This was the hardest part of his job—leaving Sasha in the middle of the night. But he needed a paycheck to clothe, feed and house himself and his eleven-year-old daughter. Natalie's parents had been in their forties when she was born and elderly by the time Sasha came along. They'd passed away while Dutch and Natalie were in college, one year apart. Dutch had only himself and his family to lean on.

A squirming warm body squeezed between Dutch and his bureau, then sat.

Rascal thumped his tail and looked at Dutch with complete adoration—and expectation.

A low chuckle forced itself past Dutch's tight throat.

"No, boy, I don't need an Australian sheepdog yip-ping around the barn with me. Wait here and keep an eye on the ladies, okay, pal?"

Rascal's fringed tail thumped twice before the dog lay down and rested his head on his front paws. His ears were still pricked, in case the tone of Dutch's voice changed. In case his master decided to take him along, after all. But he'd stopped making eye contact with Dutch. Rascal knew the deal. Birthing was vet's work, and Rascal wasn't invited.

CLAIRE GLANCED at her watch for the tenth time in as many minutes.

Where the hell was Charlie?

It was quiet, except for Stormy's heavy panting, a quiet that closed in on her. Half past two in the morning. The hour she'd always found least appealing, even when her surroundings had been the offices of the White House or a foreign capital city and not a rustic old barn with thirteen llamas.

Fourteen llamas, with one still on the way.

She left Stormy for a moment and went over to the cria, who stood in the corner of the birthing area. The surprised expression on his small face reflected her thoughts.

What the heck is going on?

"Here you go, sweetie." She crooned as she rubbed another large, dry towel over the animal in front of the heater. His shivers had ceased and he seemed more relaxed than when he'd landed on the barn floor.

Claire allowed a wave of relief to wash over her

before she returned to Stormy's side. At least one cria might make it. Her emotions reminded her of when she'd first come home to Dovetail, thinking she'd be nursing her mother through heart surgery for much longer than had turned out to be the case. Thinking she'd leave after mom got better—but deciding to stay and start her new business—the llamas.

"Hang in there, lady. Help's coming." But as she said the words Claire couldn't ignore the bitter burn of dread deep in her belly.

"No!" The cry burst up out of her.

She couldn't, *wouldn't,* lose Stormy. Stormy had been her first purchase for the farm, even before she'd found the location for Llama Fiber Haven. She'd put the money down on Stormy based on a single phone call to a couple in Michigan. They'd had to sell off their live-stock quickly due to his illness.

She recalled the conversation as though it was last night and not more than two years ago. She'd called them from location in Iraq via a satellite phone. Thirty-four days on the ground in Iraq and Afghanistan cover-ing the presidential visit had left her exhausted, grimy and on the edge of a mental breakdown. Her team was leaving the next morning, but she couldn't wait that long to talk to the llama farmers.

Her dreams of leaving Washington, D.C., and having her own business were all that kept her going by that point. Ten years of constant pressure weighed on her spirit. She'd given up everything for her job, which in the early years seemed reasonable since she could say she was doing it as a service to her country.

But she'd had nothing left for herself. She'd let all her relationships decay. First to go were her girlfriends; she couldn't possibly make time for a monthly dinner or cocktail social. Then any signs of a dating life disappeared. Her on-again, off-again relationship with a lobbyist had to be turned off permanently once she realized he wanted her to publicize his agenda.

Any new love interests never went past the second date—if they even made it that far. She'd had heads of state and diplomats, not to mention her own bosses, try to fix her up with some of their acquaintances, but it was for naught.

Claire was a dedicated career girl.

Until she had an epiphany. One that came to her, strangely enough, when she saw a group of women knitting. Claire had landed a plum interview with the First Lady during visits to local Washington charities. She'd been allowed to travel in the motorcade and should've been celebrating her journalistic coup. But then a bookstore window caught her eye. The presidential motorcade roared through D.C. unchallenged, but slowed to navigate a traffic circle.

Light glowed from the corner bookstore's front window, forming a backdrop to a group of women who sat around a table. Holding needles—knitting.

The table between them was loaded with what looked like woolen items in different colors. Sweaters? Afghans? Scarves?

But it wasn't the colors she noticed. It was the women, their oblivion to everything except what was happening around that table.

Laughing. Enjoying one another's company. Happy, living in the moment.

Claire made a lightning-swift discovery then: She didn't want to work so hard for the rest of her life, with no time for the sense of serenity the knitting women in the bookstore exuded. Even through the bulletproof glass of the limo she rode in and the windowpane of the bookstore, Claire felt the joy those women shared with one another.

She'd known in that instant that she had to go home. She'd been no more than two hours away, in Washington, D.C., for the past decade, but rural Maryland might as well have been the far side of the moon. Claire never took time off back then, not even to see her family or childhood friends.

"Ewwwwwww."

Stormy's mewl of pain brought her mind back to the present and elicited a shock of nausea. As a political reporter anxiety had been her constant companion and she'd actually believed she thrived on it.

She'd been insane.

"I'm here, Stormy." The words struggled through her dry throat as Claire stroked Stormy's long, graceful neck. Claire's stomach twisted again as she recognized that Stormy wasn't going to make it through this. Twins were too much stress on the llama's body, especially since it was her first birth.

Claire fought back tears. This was the llama who'd got her through her first year back in Dovetail. Who'd helped her start to heal over her many too-raw emotions. It felt as though Stormy was *part* of Claire.

"Hold on, Stormy! You have to."

DUTCH PULLED into the long drive that led to the farm-house Claire had purchased from the Logan family on her return to town almost two years ago. The headlights of his pickup arced across the large painted Llama Fiber Haven sign she'd erected at the end of her property, but he didn't pay attention to it. He'd already focused on the huge job that lay in front of him and the llama.

He'd managed to avoid Claire this entire time. There were at least three other vets she could go to, and had. Whenever her name or her farm came up in conversation with his colleagues, he'd been grateful he had no involvement. It was a relief that Charlie Flynn had taken her on as a full-time client.

The large-animal vets in town and surrounding environs all ran individual offices but worked together to help one another out. They had an agreement that any of them would fill in during an emergency.

Charlie was away, visiting his new grandbaby. That baby had come early, too, as the twin llama crias were arriving for Claire. The other two vets in their circle lived too far out of town to get to her place in time, so the night-duty call service had contacted Dutch.

He shook his head.

She wasn't going to be pleased when he walked into her barn.

Over the past year they'd avoided each other with all the skill of secret agents. When he'd heard she'd returned, he thought she wouldn't stay more than a few months. Claire had wanted to leave Dovetail since they were twelve and running through the sunflower fields on the south side of town. Thinking about it, he could still feel the heat of the sun on his head. Those impromptu hide-and-seek games, when they teamed up against Natalie and Tom, had been the freest time of his youth.

That was when his masculine strength was starting to surface, but before his hormones took over his motives.

He remembered how Claire used to look at him with wide-open sea-green eyes, before her curiosity and intelligence had been warped by at first an academic and then later professional drive that obliterated everything in its path. Collateral damage included Claire's best friend since toddlerhood and Dutch's deceased wife. Sasha's mother.

Natalie.

He sighed, and recalled what he'd learned in the grief support group.

"Remember to breathe."

He took in three deep breaths, exhaling completely after each one. The constant ache of loss had eased over the past three years. He still had his moments of sharp grief, but not the knee-buckling waves of it that nearly did him in during those initial months.

His resentment toward Claire, however, hadn't abated. Her lack of compassion for Natalie during Natalie's life-stealing illness was simply...unforgivable.

Especially at the end. Claire had said she'd come to see Natalie, and then didn't. She wasn't even in the country for the funeral.

"Damn it!" He pounded the leather bench seat next to him as he made the last arc up the long drive.

He had to let go of all of this, at least for the moment. He had animals to save.

CLAIRE LOOKED at her watch.

"C'mon, Charlie." Her words were hushed in the open barn. She'd renovated the space the best she could afford for her llamas, which included providing an exit for them wherever they stood. The stalls opened to the large grazing area adjacent to the barn.

She sighed and sank down on the stool she'd kept in the barn for this reason. Waiting for Stormy to give birth.

She glanced over her shoulder at the two-hour-old cria, who remained in front of the warming fan. The newborn llama watched her while it soaked up the heat from the blower. That piece of equipment had cost her several hundred dollars six months ago. Claire didn't regret a penny of it.

She'd read every agricultural manual she could get her hands on when she made the decision to leave her reporter's career in D.C. and come back here. She'd talked to countless llama and alpaca farmers on the phone and spent whole weekends on the Internet gleaning anything that would make her transition, and that of her llamas, easier.

She heard the slam of a truck door.

Finally.

She stroked the side of Stormy's neck.

"It'll be okay now, gal. Dr. Charlie's here."

At the slap of boots against the barn floor Claire looked up and saw the tall male figure at the other end of the building.

She stood.

"Over here, Charlie." She waved, then sat back down next to Stormy.

"It's not Charlie."

At the sound of his voice, she felt instant shock—and despair.

"Dutch." Her whispered response floated over the hay-strewn stall floor.

She forced herself to look at him as he approached, to keep her expression neutral.

He's not twenty anymore.

Unlike the other times she'd seen him since she'd moved back, she made herself stand tall and take in his full length. He was leaner than she remembered, more sharply defined. The barn's fluorescent lighting harshly illuminated her observations. His eyes were the same inky blue, but his hair was no longer the same shade—it was moon-silver, shockingly so. Only a small patch of blond hinted at the color it'd once been. The lines around his mouth and eyes had deepened, but not, she suspected, from laughter as much as the sorrows of his life over the past several years.

He stopped a stride away from her, his gaze steady and guarded.

"Claire." One word of greeting, but it sounded more like a condemnation.

She stood too quickly. Her knit cap slid over her eyes and she shoved it back.

"Dutch." Adolescent awkwardness returned, along with the acute awareness that she was in grimy sweats and hadn't showered since early yesterday.

She squared her shoulders and gave Dutch a glance she'd used on Afghani warlords.

Why should she even care what he thought about her?

Dutch strode over to Stormy.

"How long since the first was born?"

He was beside her, listening to Stormy's heart with his stethoscope. She had a hard time fathoming how two years of avoiding Dutch had suddenly yielded to this instant of need on the part of her animals.

"A couple of hours, from what I can guess. He was shivering when I came in here. I was surprised Stormy wasn't cleaning him, so I set up the heating fan and then I checked her. That's when I figured out she wasn't done."

"You figured right. What took you so long to call it in?"

What *had* taken her so long? She'd been so intent on following all the rules, making sure she'd be able to do this herself. She'd only called Charlie because it was a last resort. But Charlie hadn't come, Dutch had.

"I called as soon as I realized what was going on." She truly hadn't known Stormy was in labor until late last night. "Where's Charlie?"

"Away." Dutch didn't elaborate. He gave a quick look at the cria. She hated herself for studying his eyes, noticing the crinkles around them.

"You've already rubbed him down."

"Yes, I—"

"How about you continue to take care of him and I'll tend to the mother, okay?"

It was worded as the question it wasn't. At least that hadn't changed about him.

Claire massaged the cria, relieved that he seemed content to stay in the warmth of the barn and not run about in the freezing weather.

"I was worried about the temperature all day. I've been checking on Stormy every hour on the hour since late yesterday afternoon. I know llamas won't birth in bad weather if they can help it."

Dutch didn't reply. Maybe he hadn't heard her, since his concentration was focused on Stormy.

"Easy, girl. That's it." His tone was gentle yet persuasive, the perfect blend of coach and drill sergeant. Claire wondered if he'd used the same tone when Natalie gave birth to their child.

The wave of guilt at the memory of Natalie grabbed her by the throat and she coughed to cover the groan that rose up in her.

"Come over here and watch this."

Claire didn't miss that he didn't say her name.

As she watched, Dutch eased out the second cria as though he delivered breech babies all the time. He was sweating; she saw the stains under his arms. But his breathing remained steady and there was no strain in his expression. His eyes met hers for the briefest moment, and she saw a tiny flicker in their indigo depths. Of hope? Joy?

Dutch had wanted to be a vet since they were kids. He'd saved as many creatures as the Dobinsky brothers had pulled the tails off, including her beloved lizard.

"Here it is." Dutch finished delivering the second cria, but it was clear to her that this baby llama wasn't going to have as easy a time as his twin. It was much smaller and shivered constantly.

"It's a girl," Dutch murmured. "Blanket?" He reached out a gloved hand toward Claire.

She passed him one of the many clean blankets and

towels she'd stacked for this occasion. He swaddled the cria and walked it to the heater. Claire held her breath as Dutch listened through his stethoscope. She stared at his face for the slightest clue.

He removed the stethoscope from his ears and kept massaging the cria. It almost seemed too rough as far as Claire was concerned, but he was the vet. She wasn't even a llama farmer by most standards, not yet. This birth was supposed to be her stepping stone into the professional status she longed for. A breeder couldn't call herself a breeder until her animals actually had offspring.

And she'd failed.

"She's breathing. We won't know for a bit if she's going to make it." Dutch's voice was reserved, even with the grimness running through it. He didn't want to get her hopes up, or so she assumed—until she reminded herself that *her* welfare wouldn't be high in Dutch's priorities.

"What about Stormy?"

Claire kept her hand on Stormy's side as she spoke, as if by touch she could preserve the dam's will to live.

"Let me look at her. Here, come and rub this cria. Don't stop. I'll check her out."

While Claire rubbed the tiny llama, and occasionally patted its older sibling, she agonized over her stupidity. It was one thing to want to claim her farm, her business, for herself. It was quite another to put Stormy at risk.

If only she'd recognized Stormy's distress earlier last night. She'd assumed it was going to be a regular birth, just earlier than Charlie had predicted.

Stormy was more than a resource to her. She was

Claire's hope for a new future. A future that was free of the pressures of the political life she'd left behind. Free of the constant drone of the newsroom and the stress of breaking the next story.

With a start Claire realized she was perspiring more profusely than she ever had while working in the press corps. Stormy and all the rest of her llamas had at some point become more than animals to her. They were embedded in her heart.

Yet another reason to regret her decision, which had led to danger for Stormy and the two crias.

Waiting for Dutch to finish dealing with Stormy stretched Claire's anxiety to the max.

"How is she?" Claire asked the top of his silver mane. That was all she had in her line of vision.

"Shh." Dutch's admonition cut across the stable.

Claire kept rubbing the baby and decided to focus on naming the twins. They would both make it. They had to.

After what seemed like hours, but in reality wasn't more than twenty minutes, Dutch snapped off his gloves.

He made direct eye contact with Claire, and she squirmed at the intensity of his gaze. But it wasn't about her, or her and Dutch. It was about Stormy.

"She's okay for now. Her uterus is intact and the afterbirth looked normal, which is a positive sign." Dutch shook his head. "However, she's had a huge shock to her system. She won't be out of the woods for a day or so. I'm going to start her on IV antibiotics as a precaution."

"Is there any way to avoid the stronger medications? She's still young and I really don't like—"

"No, there is no other option—you made sure of that when you took this birthing on yourself. Llamas, livestock—" Dutch waved his hand around her barn "—aren't pets, Claire. They're domestic animals who serve a good purpose and need to be respected as such. They weren't put here for your entertainment."

His emotional sucker punch echoed Claire's own thoughts and drove the taste of bile into the back of her throat.

"This isn't *entertainment* for me, Dutch. These are my animals, my vocation."

She hated the electricity that quaked between them, even as they faced each other in total disgust, ignoring any remembrance of their past relationship.

"You've never been one for commitment. Is this something else to throw away when you grow tired of it?"

Her mind finished the observation: *The way you threw away your best friend? Your hometown?*

As soon as he fired the words at her and before Claire could reply, Dutch looked down.

"Damn it all to hell." He slapped the OB gloves against his thigh. After a few deep breaths, he looked back up at her.

"This has nothing to do with you, or me or our past, Claire. It has to do with your llama. If you want her to live, you need to follow my directions implicitly."

"I'm sorry—"

He held up his hand. "I'll help you until Charlie gets back—or your animals are healthy. That's it." He nodded at the firstborn cria. "He's doing okay, so I'm comfortable leaving him here. But the one you're holding—I'd rather take her back to my office to monitor."

"That could kill the mother!" Claire clutched the tiny cria as if it were her own child.

Dutch sighed. "I know. And we're shorthanded in town for the next week as far as vets go. I'll set up what you need for a llama preemie clinic right here and show you how to use the equipment. I'll drop by frequently, and you can call me anytime you need help."

He had her in the grip of his stare and she watched as his lips flattened into a thin line. "I know there was little reason for you or Charlie to expect twins—this was a rare instance for a llama birth."

He looked back at her. "No more doing *anything* with regard to your animals on your own. You're not a vet. Got it?"

Claire swallowed, but kept her mouth shut and nodded.

His gaze didn't waver from her face.

"Let's get something straight. We don't talk about our lives now, or before or whenever. Nothing personal."

"Right. Nothing personal." What else was she going to say to the man she'd hurt more than anyone—other than his dead wife?

CHAPTER TWO

SASHA LOOKED at her fairy alarm clock. Fifteen minutes until the fairy's wand hit the twelve and the alarm rang at six sharp. She reached under her bed for her cell phone to see if her best friend, Maddie, had texted her yet. They always checked to see if the other would be at the bus stop.

Her fingers brushed against a familiar organza cloth cover. The big red book.

The big red book was more of an album. It sat in a large, paper-covered box. Her mom had put it together for her before she died. When she gave Sasha the gift, Sasha was only eight. Mom had told her that someday it would help her smile and remember how much Mom loved her.

Sasha kept the box under her bed, but hadn't opened it in a while. She'd opened it a lot those first few months, that first horrible year. But since her eleventh birthday last year she hadn't looked at it as often. She still had the last photograph taken of her and Mom on her bulletin board and she looked at that every day.

In the photograph, Sasha sat on the bed next to Mom, whose head was bald, her eyes dark in her pale face. Sometimes the longing overwhelmed Sasha and she cried. But not so much anymore. She would never forget Mom, but as the years went by she was more comfortable with thinking about Mom in heaven, with no chemo, no sickness.

Sasha couldn't remember a time that her mother hadn't been sick. Maybe when she was really little, but pretty much since the end of kindergarten Mom had been seeing doctors all the time.

Sasha believed deep in her heart that Mom thought she and Dad should "move on" and get their lives going without worrying about what Mom would think. She wasn't planning to ask Dad about this—he was too busy with the vet business and now he was worried because Aunt Ginny had to go away to law school and Sasha would be Without a Female Mentor.

A knock at her door startled her.

"Sasha, are you up? You have to take your shower *now.*"

Sasha glanced at her fairy alarm clock.

She'd stayed in bed ten minutes longer than usual.

"Okay, Aunt Ginny, I'm up."

"YOU LOOK LIKE HELL." Dottie Vasquez made the observation as she poured Dutch his third cup of coffee.

"We can't all look as good as you at six in the morning." He mustered a smile for the woman who owned the diner. Dottie was his mother's age, but had the spirit of a teenager.

She smiled back at him. "No, but I've seen you looking better, Dutch." She put the coffeepot on the burner, then returned to chat. The breakfast rush was over for

the early farmers, and she had a few minutes' rest before
the next wave of customers came in. Dutch knew this
was what Dottie liked more than serving coffee or food
to hungry people. She liked to talk—and to listen.

"Word is, the lights were on at the Llama Haven
all night."

Dutch met Dottie's blue eyes, still bright even sur-
rounded by crow's-feet. "I swear, Dot, I hope the U.S.
government knows where to come when they need information about anything. Do you ever miss a beat?"

His banter didn't distract Dottie.

"With Charlie and Missy out of town," she said, referring to the other vet and his wife, "I figured you
were over there tending to a birth. Does Dovetail have
a new baby llama?"

"As a matter of fact, it has two." He sipped his coffee.
He usually had one or two cups in the morning—his
work gave him enough of a jump start. But today he'd
needed more.

"Twins?" Dottie's eyebrows rose and her next question formed on her lips but the diner door flew open and
a crowd of truckers tumbled in.

"Hold that thought, Dutch. I want the details."

Dottie got the crew settled. After she'd put her top
waitress on the job, she came back to the counter. Dutch
considered using the opportunity to escape, but didn't.
Dottie was harmless and had listened to many of his
woes over the years. She was nice to Sasha, too.

But she didn't sit down next to him again. The diner
was hopping with hungry customers.

"Twins?"

Dutch stood and met her gaze. "Yeah, twins—and I'm not sure the little one's going to make it. I need to get back out there and check up on her."

"I imagine it's easier for you and Claire to get along when you both have something to focus on."

Dottie didn't have to explain. Dutch knew.

Other than yourselves, your history.

He shrugged on his coat, pulled out his wallet.

"Exactly." He put down the money, as always with a generous tip. Dutch appreciated being able to stay in a small town and raise his daughter here, and he was more than willing to pay for it. He knew Dottie had lost business since they put in that big national franchise breakfast place off the highway, but she'd kept her prices reasonable and still served the best coffee this side of Chesapeake Bay.

"See you later, Dot."

"See you."

Dutch walked out into the parking lot and looked up at the sky. There was nothing like a Maryland sunrise, and today's had been no exception. The last remaining streaks of pink and purple faded into the clear sky, harbinger of another cold, windy day.

He got into the front seat of his truck and glanced at the clock as he switched on the ignition. If he was lucky he'd make it home in time to sit with Sasha through her breakfast.

Then he'd have to return to check on the cria. And face Claire's wary green eyes, her hesitant behavior around him.

"Good. Keeps her on her toes," he muttered to himself as he turned into his driveway.

"SASHA, TIME TO get out!" Sasha heard Aunt Ginny's voice through the bathroom door and turned off the shower.

"Okay!" Sasha buried her face in her towel.

She was going to miss Aunt Ginny, who'd told Sasha last week that it was time for all of them to move on. Dutch was Aunt Ginny's older brother, but she'd been like a big sister to him and Sasha these past few years.

At first, Sasha didn't like it when Aunt Ginny had said their house felt like Mom was still here. Ginny had come to live with them toward the end of Natalie's life, when hospice had taken over, and Sasha remembered spending lots of time with her aunt. But lately Sasha had started thinking maybe Aunt Ginny was right. Her friends whose parents were divorced had either bought new houses or fixed up their old ones. And they got new husbands or wives.

Daddy didn't act as though he ever wanted a new wife, not even a girlfriend. He said he never wanted to forget Mom. Neither did Sasha.

But a new mom might not be so bad.

She had distinct memories of Mom and of her dying—the days Mom spent lying on the couch and on what Sasha knew was a hospital bed. But somehow Aunt Ginny had helped it not be too sad. Sasha remembered the times when no one could stop the sad stuff. Like when Mom had bad reactions to the medicine or when it got really close to the end and all she did was sleep. She seemed to fade away that last summer.

Sasha was so glad Aunt Ginny had stayed. She was going to miss her, but she was also looking forward to being alone with Dad. Whenever Aunt Ginny had to go to Baltimore or on trips with her study group, Sasha had liked the father-daughter time with Dad. Plus she loved being with him on his job. She loved animals at least as much as he did.

Sasha hurried down the stairs and hit the wide-plank pine flooring of the hallway. Rascal clipped along beside her, trying to herd her into the kitchen.

"Good morning, sunshine!" Aunt Ginny met her halfway and hugged her tight. Sasha was eleven, almost twelve, but never tired of Aunt Ginny's hugs or kisses.

Aunt Ginny pulled back a bit and looked into Sasha's eyes. Aunt Ginny had Dad's deep blue eyes, which Sasha often wished she had, too. Instead, she'd inherited her Mom's brown eyes, which Dad and Aunt Ginny told her were beautiful and she'd be grateful for when she got older.

"What?" She hated it when Aunt Ginny looked at her for too long.

"How are you today? Good?"

"Yeah." Sasha squirmed out of Aunt Ginny's arms and went over to the counter. Someone had cleaned it up and put all the appliances away.

"Where's the toaster?" Aunt Ginny never put things back in the same place twice.

"Under the counter. I bought some cinnamon waffles yesterday."

"Thanks!" Sasha loved it when Aunt Ginny did the grocery shopping. Dad was more practical and would've bought plain waffles or no waffles at all—just some regular bread for toasting.

Sasha saw all the thick books Aunt Ginny had on the breakfast counter.

"Are you still studying?" She thought Aunt Ginny's exams were over.

"I'm reviewing. When I start law school, I'll be expected to be on top of all these subjects."

"Huh." Sasha enjoyed school and homework, but didn't know how adults stayed awake when they were reading such thick books with all that small type.

Aunt Ginny was almost done with her bachelor's degree. She'd done it from Dovetail, going into College Park as needed. Dad said Aunt Ginny had made a Great Sacrifice for them. Now she had to go live in Baltimore and go to the university there for law school. She'd be leaving soon to attend a spring review class before courses started at the end of the summer.

"Where's Daddy?" Sasha spread peanut butter on her waffle. Aunt Ginny had sat down with her coffee and books.

"He got a late-night call."

As soon as the words were out, Rascal whimpered and ran to the kitchen door. Sasha heard the slam as her dad got out of his truck.

"Daddy!" Sasha went over to the door as Dutch opened it and jumped at him. He wrapped his arms around her and gave her a hug.

"Hi, sweetheart. You smell like a bunch of flowers." He tugged at Sasha's still-damp hair.

"It's the shampoo Aunt Ginny got for me last Christmas."

"Is it?"

Sasha nodded, then finished making her breakfast. Dad looked tired—his eyes were deep in his face and the lines around them made him seem like he was squinting.

"What happened?" Aunt Ginny must have noticed, too.

"Twin llama birth. One's fine, the mother will hopefully be okay, but I don't know about the second one. She's really small and it's going to be touch and go for a few days."

"Can I go see them with you?"

"No." Dutch's response was immediate and it hurt. She *hated* when he was like this.

"Well, excuse me." She shoved a bite of waffle into her mouth.

She heard her dad sigh, then he walked back to her.

"I'm sorry, Sash." He tousled her hair. "I've been up all night, and I haven't had an easy time of it. Of course you can go see the llamas, but not today. Let's give them all a chance to settle in, okay?"

"Sure." Sasha took her waffle and sat on a stool at the counter. "Do you want a waffle, Daddy?"

"No, thanks, sugarplum. I ate at Dot's, before you were even out of bed. But I'll sit with you, if that's okay."

"Okay. Wait! Let me go get my essay that I'm handing in today. You can read it over for me." Sasha ran up the back stairs to her room. She heard Aunt Ginny laugh at her excitement.

What were they going to do when Aunt Ginny wasn't there to calm Dad down?

GINNY TURNED to Dutch, before Sasha bounded back into the kitchen.

"How'd it go?"

Dutch screwed up his face and frowned at his baby sister, who looked so innocent with her widened eyes and lifted brows. But he knew she wasn't asking about the llamas, not really.

"Fine. Awful. I hated it. I'm glad I saved the twin and, I hope, the dam." He stared down at the floor.

"I can't look at that woman without remembering, without seeing the pain on Natalie's face when her calls weren't returned."

"I know." Ginny's voice was soft. She'd seen it, too. Claire and Natalie had been closer than sisters through grade school and high school. The only thing that had ever come between them was a boy.

Dutch.

"I don't get it, Ginny. How someone so smart can be so stupid, especially with her friend, her family." He couldn't believe he was sharing so much with Ginny, but he blamed it on exhaustion.

"Sounds like she's learned something," Ginny said, giving him a level gaze. "She quit the press corps when her mom got sick, helped her mother through her heart surgery, and she's stayed here even though she doesn't need to anymore. She's serious about making a go of it, Dutch. It's been two years already."

"Trust me, Ginny, if Claire Renquist has stayed in Dovetail, or anywhere, it's for her benefit and hers alone. Claire doesn't do anything solely for others. That part of her died a long time ago." He snorted.

If it ever existed.

Ginny laughed, but not with any hint of sarcasm.

"Do you want some lemon with those bitters? Jeeze, Dutch, let it go. Some people *do* change."

He grunted. He wanted to say "not Claire" but Ginny had a point. He'd turned into a crusty old man at the age of thirty-four.

Ginny had been a kid when Dutch and Claire dated, and not much older when they broke up. Dutch had married Natalie right out of college. He'd only recently told Ginny that he and Natalie had a pregnancy scare way back in high school after that fateful night during senior year. The night that ended any remaining relationship he'd had with Claire and permanently ruined Natalie and Claire's childhood bond.

"Look, Daddy." Sasha, back downstairs, slid onto the stool next to Dutch. He read her essay with one arm around her. He loved the fact that she still snuggled close, their two heads bent over the paper, the comfortable intimacy between daughter and dad.

Dutch knew he needed to learn to be comfortable with other people, too. It was more than three years now—Natalie was at peace, and he wanted to find some peace for himself.

He looked up at Ginny as she watched him and Sasha. He could read her mind.

They'd been alone too long, he and Sasha.

"Don't get any ideas, Ginny." He tried to act as if he was focused on Sasha's essay, but few knew him better than Ginny.

"What kind of ideas?" Sasha piped in.

"Matchmaking ideas, honey." Ginny sipped her coffee. "Your dad's worried I'll try to set him up with someone." Ginny rolled her eyes.

"Do you mean like on a date?" Sasha's interested was piqued.

"This is adult conversation, Sasha." Dutch stared hard at Ginny. He loved his kid sister, but she was like every other female when it came to romance.

She thought everyone needed it.

Ginny, of course, ignored him. "Yes, Sasha, like a date," she said. "Your dad could benefit from adult female companionship."

"Ginny!" Dutch growled, but the edge in his voice masked the nervous twist in his gut. What did he have to be anxious about? Ginny was the one acting weird.

"Don't 'Ginny' me, Dutch. Sasha's old enough to understand this conversation, aren't you, honey?"

"Yup!" Sasha's head bobbed enthusiastically. She looked sideways at Dutch. The female gleam in her eyes made him laugh in spite of himself.

"Aunt Ginny's right, Dad. You need a woman."

CHAPTER THREE

"SHE'S DOING as well as I could hope. It could still go either way, but she's a tough gal, aren't you, Stormy?"

Dutch patted the llama's side and his voice lowered to a soft lilt. He kept his gaze on the llama. Claire's breath caught.

Here was the Dutch she'd known as a teen. Caring, assured, comfortable with his intelligence and ability. She watched his hands stroke Stormy and couldn't stop the memory of how those hands had felt on *her* when they were lovesick teenagers.

On that hot, breezy summer afternoon in Ocean City. When all that mattered was Dutch and the love they'd discovered, the love that went beyond their childhood friendship. When she knew she'd never love anyone as much as she loved him at that moment.

Dutch must have felt her stare just now as he looked up and their eyes met. She saw his recognition of her, not as the girl who'd run out of town, not as the woman who'd broken her best friend's heart, but as Claire.

It was Dutch and Claire. That connection still seared her thoughts. Her awareness belied the notion that the energy between them was a mere relic of their past. Whatever their connection, it was real and alive. Today.

The heat between them caught her off guard.

Dutch blinked and she watched the immediate judgment flood back into his expression. How many layers of disgust toward her did he harbor?

Not more than she harbored toward herself.

"Thanks, Dutch." She broke the silence abruptly.

"No thanks needed. I'll check on her again tonight." Dutch gave the cria a quick exam and straightened up.

"She seems to be doing fine." She offered up the observation in an attempt to mask her awareness of him.

Dutch glanced at her for the briefest of moments. "Yeah, I'm not worried about her. You were smart to have the heater on hand." His grudging expression reflected his sincerity.

"At least I did one thing right."

"Spare me the martyr act, Claire."

He put his hat on and picked up his bags. "I'll come by before dinnertime."

He turned and strode out of the barn. Claire was glad he didn't look back at her. She wasn't sure she was keeping the sorrow off her face.

She had to force herself to focus on the positive. Claire had thought she'd already done that when she started this new venture. It wasn't easy, beginning a llama fiber business. Once she had the llamas, she'd needed to find someone to spin the fleece into yarn. She'd been lucky to come across a small business that spun yarn commercially and by hand, so she could please her future customers.

Other aspects of running the farm had also fallen into place, and Claire's confidence had bloomed.

Until Dutch walked into the barn to save her llamas that dark night.

DUTCH WAITED for Sasha in front of the middle school. She'd entered sixth grade this past autumn and, with it, middle school. When he'd been growing up he sure didn't recall the girls looking the way Sasha wanted to dress. She was eleven going on twenty-five, and it scared the hell out of him.

Sasha's face lit up when she saw him standing there, and he turned to get into the truck ahead of her. A couple of years ago he'd wait for her, hugging her when she grabbed him in a fierce greeting. But now she didn't like him to be visible if she was in public. He knew from what Ginny told him that this was all normal, but it still gave him a punch in the gut.

Sasha was all he had. Ginny was getting ready to leave; she'd been accepted into law school. And she *should* leave, she had every right to—she had her own life to lead. But with Sasha entering puberty and adolescence, he knew he was going to miss Ginny's steady presence. The security she provided as an adult woman in Sasha's life. What was he going to do without Ginny when Sasha got her period?

He could call his mother, but he didn't see Sasha as willing to talk to her grandmother Archer about her body's changes. His parents had been a fantastic support for Sasha and him through the grieving, but they were active seniors now, with lives of their own. He couldn't ask them to help raise another child.

"Hi, Daddy."

"Hi, honey." He leaned over and gave her a quick peck on the cheek, which she reciprocated. When was *this* going to end? He hoped never.

"How was school?"

"Fine. Mr. Ignacio wore this really weird sweater today—it had frogs on it."

"Frogs?" Mr. Ignacio was the sixth-grade science teacher and he marched to his own formula, from what Sasha told him.

"Yeah. Then Joey said it looked dumb, and Mr. Ignacio said, 'Yeah, well, I think wearing a company's advertising for them is dumb.'"

"Was Joey wearing a logo shirt?"

"Yeah, and these really expensive sneakers, too." Sasha chattered the entire way home. Most of the time he ended up tuning some of it out. How on earth did she keep such detailed but inconsequential information about her teachers and friends in her brain, much less repeat it over and over?

"Dad? Daaad!"

"Oops. Sorry, honey." His attention had been on the road.

"So can I?"

"Can you what?"

"Sleep over at Naomi's? Maddie might be able to go, too, and it would give you a break."

"Uh, no, not tonight." Not *any* night, not since he'd heard that Naomi's mother was picked up for a DUI. He had to award Sasha points on the manipulation attempt, though.

"Come on, Dad."

"No." He was grateful that Natalie had taught him to be consistent with Sasha since she was a toddler. She pretty much accepted "no" without too much resistance. For the most part.

"Fine." She sighed, the weight of it bearing resignation and youthful angst.

I'm such a mean parent.

"What's for dinner?"

"What do you want?" Fridays were their evenings together, another reason Dutch didn't want Sasha going to a friend's house. He enjoyed their movie and popcorn nights and was reluctant to let go of them.

"Can we have tacos?"

He groaned inside. His stomach couldn't take much fast food anymore. But Sasha loved the drive-through, and he could get himself a salad.

"Why don't we go now and pick them up? It's a little early, but that'll give us room for popcorn and ice cream later on."

"All right!" Sasha nodded her approval, the missed sleepover apparently forgotten.

THEY ATE FROM the wrappers at the kitchen table, both devouring the early meal. Dutch looked up at the clock.

"I have to go check on some patients, but I'll only be gone a half an hour or so. Think you can keep yourself out of trouble for that long?"

He'd been trusting her alone a little at a time, since she was approaching her twelfth birthday. Ginny had gone to her usual weekend prelaw study night in Baltimore, and he still had to visit the llamas.

"Where are you going?"

"I need to take a quick look at the llamas."

As soon as the words left his mouth he knew he'd made a mistake. Sasha homed in for the kill.

"Daddy, you *promised* I could go the next time you visit a llama farm. And it's only fair 'cause you didn't let me go to the sleepover."

His jaw tightened. He didn't want Sasha anywhere near Claire.

Too dangerous. Too many questions.

The answers are what you're afraid of.

"I don't think so, Sasha, not tonight."

He heard the unreasonable tone in his voice, but it was too late to soften his delivery. Sasha's face fell, then reddened with emotion.

"Stop treating me like a baby, Dad! I won't get in the way or cause you any problems."

"I know that, sweetheart." He expelled a breath, giving in. "Okay, you can come along. But it's going to be a quick visit, so don't think you're staying with the llamas all night."

"I won't." She pulled on her hat and gloves as she spoke and he felt the dread gather inside him.

Anything would be better than going back to Claire's—especially with Sasha.

CHAPTER FOUR

CLAIRE HEARD the truck pull in, the crunch of gravel and the slam of doors.

Doors?

She looked out the window and saw the person who'd accompanied Dutch. A small, thin figure walked beside him, shadowing his moves.

His and Natalie's daughter.

Claire let the curtain fall. She'd planned on staying in, poking her head out when Dutch came back from the barn, keeping their conversation to a minimum.

But he'd brought his daughter.

Their daughter.

Natalie hadn't gotten pregnant after she and Dutch made love that fateful night in high school, while Claire was away. They'd had a scare when her period was late. And the fallout from that scare put the lid on the coffin that held Dutch and Claire's dying relationship.

What hurt the most was that Dutch and Natalie had stayed together after the scare and Dutch's one-night indiscretion. Dutch and Natalie had gone to college together, married and had a child. Dutch's night with Natalie hadn't been just a one-night stand, although that was what they'd both told her in those dark days of senior year.

It was a long time ago, she reminded herself.

Claire wondered if she'd made a mistake in assuming she'd never get over the emotional trauma Dutch and Natalie's relationship had inflicted on her. Maybe if she'd come clean with Natalie all those years ago and told her they couldn't be friends anymore...

But back when they were in grade school, Claire and Natalie had promised each other they'd *always* be friends. In high school they'd watched other girls fight and lose lifelong friendships over boys and swore that would never happen to them.

But it had. And instead of leveling with Natalie, Claire had told her she was over Dutch and happy for Natalie, and the two of them would remain friends.

It had worked for a while. Claire came back from college for weekends and spent time with Natalie. It was better when Dutch wasn't around, which had been often. When he was, Claire never spoke to him if she could avoid it. More importantly, she never allowed herself to be alone with him.

Except the night of Natalie's bachelorette party.

Claire groaned at the humiliating memory.

After that, Claire had kept up her charade of friendship-as-usual as long as she could. But when the baby came, and Dutch and Natalie were a no-kidding family, Claire found she didn't have the energy to put on her show of indifference anymore. She'd loved Natalie, but had to save the few scraps of self-respect she had left. She'd seen Sasha once, as an infant at

Natalie's belated baby shower; she'd never spent time with her again.

If she was smart she'd continue that approach and stay in the house.

Her thoughts warred with her curiosity. Curiosity won. What kind of girl had Dutch and Natalie's baby become?

Claire threw on her merino cardigan, shoved the wool cap she'd just finished knitting onto her head and went out the back door. The afternoon air hung heavy with the threat of rain. As she entered the barn, she saw the gray clouds through the open stalls. They served as a perfect backdrop for the young girl in her periwinkle jacket.

If Claire expected an immediate earth-shattering recognition of Dutch and Natalie's daughter, it didn't happen.

Sasha stood quietly off to the side, smiling at the smallest cria. Dutch examined Stormy with the same focus she'd seen this morning. He was a gifted vet; she had to give him that. He knew his job and he didn't permit any distractions.

Claire walked toward them, her footsteps virtually silent on the hay-strewn ground. She wore her favorite barn shoes—slip-on suede mules with supportive rubber soles. Hand-knit socks from the local yarn store kept her feet warm. She looked forward to the day when she'd be able to knit her own socks.

"Hello," Claire greeted the girl.

Dutch didn't respond as he tended to Stormy. But his daughter met Claire's gaze with uncompromising candor. Just like Natalie would have done.

"Hi. I'm Sasha, Dr. Archer's daughter."

"I'm Claire."

Sasha stared at her and Claire thought she saw a question in Sasha's huge brown eyes. But none came.

"You look like your mom."

"You knew my mom?" Claire cringed at the hopeful expression on Sasha's face. *Great.* She should've kept her mouth shut.

"That was years ago, Sasha, before you were born." Dutch's voice cut across the stable, but it didn't appear to affect Sasha as it did Claire. Claire wanted to climb over the slats and run for the hills.

"Huh. So you went to school with her? Have you always lived in Dovetail?"

"No, yes… I mean, yes, I lived here as a child, then left for school." Complete with a broken heart.

"I know who you are!" Sasha stepped closer. "You're the TV reporter who came back because you had nowhere else to go."

"That's one way of putting it."

Claire slipped her hands in her pockets. Why had she allowed her curiosity to bring her out here? She would've been more comfortable in the dentist chair getting a root canal.

"So you *did* know my mom—she used to point you out on TV. You look a lot different now."

Claire couldn't help laughing.

"I don't dress like that anymore, and my hair's longer." She'd abandoned her expensive coif the minute she'd left the press corps. She'd had a few trims in the past year, and her former chin-length bob had grown past her shoulders and was wavy now. No more blow-dried-straight haircuts. She wanted to be herself.

Whoever *herself* was.

"I gave Stormy an extra shot of anti-inflammatory. She's doing okay, but I don't like how swollen she still is." Dutch's deep voice interrupted them and Claire welcomed the reprieve.

Claire bit her lip. She wanted him and his daughter out of here. It was bad enough finally meeting Sasha, but to have Dutch observe the event…

This could've been our daughter.

She blew the thought out of her mind as quickly as it'd blown in. Life hadn't worked out the way they'd expected. But it wasn't fair to involve Sasha in any of it.

As Dutch went over to examine the crias, Sasha stared at her with unnerving intensity.

"Did someone make that hat for you?"

Claire's hand jerked to her head. "It's a beret."

Sasha kept staring. "The ribbing's messed up. That's why it keeps slipping down past your eyes."

Claire swiped the hat off her head and looked at it in the barn's fluorescent light. The creation she'd planned to knit, modeled after a hat she'd seen in the local yarn store, didn't measure up to her own expectations, either.

"It's a blend of llama and merino wools. The hand-painted color is supposed to give it a variegated appearance."

"You *did* make it, didn't you?" Sasha was more effective than a lot of the journalists Claire had worked with. The kid wouldn't let up.

Claire raised her eyebrows. "Yes, I did. I haven't

been knitting that long, and it's my first finished project."

"Where did you learn?"

"To knit?" Claire stalled. Now came the pathetic truth about her circumstances. "I taught myself."

"From what?"

"A book. Internet videos."

"Did you know knitters sometimes get together at bookstores? There's a group that meets every Thursday at the store in Annapolis."

Yes, Claire knew that knitters met in bookstores, and she knew about the Annapolis group in particular. She'd already been there. Once. They'd all but ignored her. There were members from all over Maryland, but the core group was from Dovetail. The women in this group remembered her as the girl who left. They remembered Natalie, too.

Another way this small town was keeping her at arm's length. She didn't want to resign herself to the status of "Natalie's horrible best friend" so she abandoned the group after just one visit, along with any intention of trying it again. Victim wasn't a role Claire had ever been fond of playing.

"I'm usually very busy with the llamas."

Sasha smiled. "It's fun. Or at least that's what my friends' moms say."

"Maybe I'll try it sometime." Claire watched how Sasha kept looking at her hat.

"So, you knit?" Claire tossed the question at her.

"A little. My mom taught me, and Aunt Ginny tries to help me every now and then, but I'm better than she is."

So Natalie had been a knitter. Claire remembered

when they'd both gone through a brief crocheting phase, but had dropped that in favor of beading.

A wave of nostalgia overwhelmed her with memories she'd pushed down so far she thought she'd forgotten them. Staring at Natalie's daughter certainly added to the poignancy of her recollections.

"Are you okay?"

"Hmm?" Claire shook her head and refocused her gaze on Sasha. "Yes, I'm fine."

"You're crushing your hat."

Claire forced her hands to relax their grip. Sasha's bold assessment should've made her laugh, since it was the same kind of attitude Natalie had possessed, an attitude that had made Claire laugh many times. But Claire felt her heart constrict. Sasha wasn't Natalie, and Natalie wasn't coming back.

"So, do you want to be a vet like your dad?"

Sasha wrinkled up her nose. "Not really. I don't know. I love animals, of course, but I think I may want to be a lawyer."

"A lawyer? My sister's studying to be a lawyer."

Sasha nodded. "She knows my aunt Ginny. They're going to be in the same class. Aunt Ginny's moving to Baltimore next week so she can take refresher courses or something."

"I bet you'll miss her." It was common knowledge that Dutch's sister had lived with him and Sasha since Natalie became too sick to care for herself. She'd stayed on after Natalie had passed away.

"Yeah, we'll miss her. But Aunt Ginny needs to have her own life."

Claire smiled. Sasha was obviously repeating what Dutch had told her, but she said it with such conviction, as if the words were her own.

"Hey, look!" Sasha's joy-filled squeal startled Claire. Sasha pointed at the twin crias, who'd decided to jump around their pen as though it was seven in the morning and not evening.

"They're a pair, all right," Claire said. "The little one's obviously improving. They've started to play together."

"I want to get their picture." Sasha reached into one jacket pocket, then the other, and frowned.

"Dad, I forgot my camera!"

Dutch looked at her from the side bench. He'd finished his exams and was packing up his kit.

"Sorry, kiddo. Better luck next time."

Sasha giggled. "So I'll come out with you tomorrow on your evening rounds, right? And we can bring Rascal with us?"

Claire stifled the laugh that rolled up her throat at Dutch's pained expression. Clearly, Sasha's spending time at Llama Fiber Haven was *not* in his game plan.

Dutch lowered his eyebrows and looked at Sasha. "We'll talk about it later."

"Okay." Sasha turned back to Claire. "What are their names?"

"I have no idea. I keep trying to come up with something. So far nothing's stuck." She didn't want to tell Sasha that she wasn't completely sure the younger cria was going to make it, and with Stormy still at risk, naming the twins wasn't a priority.

"Why don't you name them now?" Sasha watched the baby llamas, her eyes full of sparkle and life. Claire wondered if her own eyes had ever been that young.

"Well…" Claire hedged. Dutch was almost done—maybe she could put off the naming until Sasha came back. She'd be ready for both of them next time, perhaps even have a treat for Sasha. Especially with Ginny moving, Sasha might enjoy some pampering. Claire knew Sasha probably had more than enough attention from Dutch's parents, but now that Sasha had identified Claire as one of her mother's childhood friends, it would be nice to offer Sasha some comfort.

"Look! He keeps nipping at her side, to get her to play." Sasha giggled again. "And she tucks her head in and hides from him."

"Until she decides to give him a kick—she did earlier today." Claire laughed at Sasha's infectious enthusiasm.

"Why don't you call them Nip and Tuck?" the girl suggested.

"Sounds good to me." Claire turned back to the llamas. "Hey, Tuck, stop bothering Nip!" She smiled at Sasha. "Perfect."

"Hey, Nip, go ahead and kick Tuck!" Sasha got into the act and stepped closer to Claire. Claire looked down at her new friend. Same hair color as Natalie, same wit as Dutch. But Sasha was very much her own person. Dutch was going to have his hands full raising her through the teenage years.

Claire looked up from Sasha and over at the llamas. Her eyes caught on the brilliant blue gaze that pinned her from across the barn. Dutch was angry, but she didn't think it was at her as much as the situation. Claire sent him a slow smile, which only made his brows draw closer together over his strong nose.

Let him be angry. He had to learn sooner or later that he couldn't control everything. He might have issues with Claire, but apparently his daughter didn't. And wasn't Sasha's well-being his primary concern?

CHAPTER FIVE

"SO YOU CAN HELP me out?" Two days later, Claire looked at Jewel and Jenna, her twenty-two-year-old twin sisters. They sat in their parents' kitchen. Fred and Dona Renquist had gone out shopping. Jewel and Jenna were still living at home until they started their individual graduate programs.

Claire met the twins every week whenever they weren't away at college. Now they'd both graduated and had some time on their hands before graduate school. In fact, Jewel had decided to move back until she entered her Physical Therapy program. Jenna was going right into law school.

"I have six months until I begin working on my physical-therapy degree. I've got an internship at the clinic, but it's only part-time. I'll be here for the Sheep and Wool Festival—and I can help you with starting up the yarn shop. It'll be a nice break for me." Jewel grabbed one of Dona's pecan cookies, which she'd taken from the freezer. Mom always froze extra batches she'd baked so the girls could take them out to thaw and enjoy.

Claire looked at Jenna. "Are you sure you can take time off for this?"

"The Sheep and Wool Festival is just one weekend, right?" Jenna sipped her iced tea.

"Yes, but I need help on Thursday, then I need someone to work shifts with me so I know the llamas are safe from overexcited festival attendees."

"Count me in." Jenna smiled at her older sister.

Sitting around Mom and Dad's kitchen table made the years fade. If Claire closed her eyes, she could still see the whole family here, meal after meal.

"It's great that you two want to help me. I'd ask Mom and Dad, but their cruise starts Sunday and they fly out Saturday night."

Fred and Dona were buying new luggage today.

The twins smiled. Even at twenty-two they were undeniably linked more than average siblings. They shared Claire's green eyes, but had straight, bright red hair instead of Claire's wavy blond.

Both Fred and Dona were teachers; Dona still taught sixth grade, and Fred high school mathematics. During their spring break, they'd decided to take themselves on a cruise.

Claire laughed. "I wonder if they're fighting over what color luggage to buy."

"Doubtful." Jenna grinned. "As long as Mom's happy, Dad is, too. Odds are he lets her pick whatever she wants. He intends to set the mood for a romantic Caribbean cruise."

Jewel held up her hands. "I don't want to hear any details."

"Me, either." Jenna shook her head.

"I agree, no details. But we're really lucky that Mom

and Dad have each other and that they're still happy after all these years and everything they've been through." Claire leaned back in the oak chair. It was hard to believe that only a couple of years ago their mother had needed major heart surgery.

"When Mom got sick, none of us had to help nearly as much as we might have. Since Dad went through cardiac rehab, he knew what she needed." Claire felt it was her duty to be the voice of reason.

"Yeah, and it's obvious to me that Mom recovered so quickly because she has Dad." Jewel peered out the window at the plethora of bird feeders Dona had arranged on the back deck. "Look, two robins mating!"

Claire and Jenna groaned. Jewel always seemed to find the romance in every situation.

"Speaking of mating, Claire, what's going on with you and Dutch?" Jenna took advantage of the moment to ask what Claire was sure she and Jewel had been thinking about all morning.

"What do you mean? He filled in for Charlie while he was gone."

The twins exchanged a glance. "So why's he still hanging out at your place?"

"It's purely professionalism. Dutch has simply been following up on the llamas' health. He birthed the crias, so it's only natural that he'd want to keep caring for them." She hoped she didn't sound defensive.

"Yeah! I heard he's been bringing his daughter around, too." Jenna smirked.

"You never told me!" Jewel slapped Jenna's arm. "Yeah, Claire. What's going on?"

Claire rolled her eyes. "I do love being back here, but this is one part I didn't miss." She referred to what she called the girl-in-the-fishbowl syndrome. Anything that happened in Dovetail stayed in Dovetail and on everybody's wagging tongues.

"You're stalling, Claire. Give us the goods." Jewel was not letting this go.

Claire took her time, breaking off half a cookie and chasing it with lemon water.

"Dutch brought his daughter, Sasha, over to meet the llamas," she eventually said. "Sasha and I hit it off. They've been to visit maybe half a dozen times. She loves the animals."

Claire kept to the facts, as the twins were bound to read volumes into each word.

"Ginny's on her way to law school at the University of Baltimore—" she nodded at Jenna "—with you. Sasha's going to be lonely for an older female in her life—and it's nice that I can provide some of Natalie's history."

Claire took another bite of her cookie, astonished that neither Jewel nor Jenna had interrupted her musing.

"Sasha's at an age where she's naturally curious about what her mother was like at eleven or twelve." She glanced at each twin in turn. "Since Natalie and I were inseparable at that age, it makes sense for me to be in her life right now. And I want to be. It's a way of bringing back some good memories." She splayed her hands on the kitchen table. "It's also giving me a chance to make things up to Natalie. To make up for the time I wasn't here when she was sick."

"How's Dutch taking it? He must be mad that Sasha likes you, in spite of what you—"

Jenna visibly clamped her mouth shut. Jewel shot her twin a glowering look. Too late. Claire could already feel the wounds in her heart start to seep.

Jewel tried to cover for her blunder. "In spite of missing her mother, I mean."

Claire gave them a wry smile. "Actually, Sasha isn't so wrapped up in Natalie at this point. Yes, Natalie was her mother and she'll never forget her. But I get the impression that she's ready to move on, that she doesn't want to be grieving her mother all the time." The way Dutch still did.

"So Dutch is letting go of his resentment?"

"Are you sure you want to get involved with them?"

Both twins spoke at once.

Claire released a short laugh. "No, it's clear to me that Dutch isn't letting go as much as he probably should. But who am I to judge? It's none of my business."

Jewel and Jenna shared a "she's only kidding herself" look.

"Don't you think you could make a difference? You and Dutch *did* have something once." Jewel turned back to Jenna for help.

"Yes, when you were in high school I thought you were going to marry him after graduation, or at least after college." Jenna raised her brows for effect.

"You guys were eight years old. What did you know?"

"Not as much as we know today, and today we know that the whole town's talking about how Dutch looks since he's been taking care of your llamas. When we ran into Ginny in Baltimore she told us that his positive attitude's come back. That's huge, Claire. He's been the grouch around here for over three years."

"Longer if you count when Natalie got sick," Jenna added.

"I should've known you'd talk to Ginny." Claire looked at her younger sisters, shaking her head.

"Ginny talked to *us*. Saw us at the university open house and filled us in. She's doing a refresher course before her courses begin. It's really hard for her to finally leave for law school, but she's already sacrificed, what, two years?"

Claire sighed. "I'm not doing this for Dutch or Ginny. Like I said, I'm doing it for Natalie, but, most importantly, for Sasha." As she spoke, an incredible certainty came over her.

All along she'd thought that somehow she would make up for her behavior with Natalie. She'd never expected it would be through Natalie's daughter, but the opportunity was staring her in the face.

"What about *you* and Dutch, Claire? Natalie's been gone for years now."

"Maybe three years sounds like a long time to you, but I'm sure Dutch would beg to differ."

"Seriously, Claire, what's keeping you two from at least having fun together?" Jenna was so fresh faced and naive in her query that Claire laughed.

"There's nothing between Dutch and me. Cool it."

"But you two were best friends for ages! And the four of you—Dutch, Natalie, you and Tom," Jenna said, referring to Natalie's twin brother, "were inseparable my entire childhood."

"You and Dutch *did* date in high school, I remember!"

Yes, they had dated. More than date—as Jenna observed; Claire had believed she and Dutch were forging a basis for the rest of their lives. Until one night when Dutch's efforts to comfort Natalie turned into lovemaking...

You're not being fair. You'd already created a huge rift with your college plans.

"Yeah, but we broke up when Dutch and Natalie got...involved." Claire's hands started to itch, and the room felt unseasonably warm.

"You mean when he thought he got her pregnant." Jenna, always the more practical of the twins, spat out the statement.

"That's old history."

"I never understood why you two never got back together. I mean, Natalie *wasn't* pregnant, and they didn't get married right away. Why didn't you and Dutch ever work things out?"

"Our time had passed. I was going to conquer the world, Dutch had vet school ahead of him and Natalie planned to get her B.A. and her master's in history so she could be an archivist for the state." She stifled another deep sigh. Fatigue overwhelmed her.

"Dutch had fallen in love with Natalie," Claire went on. "And she fell for him, too. They were meant to be together at that point." She stated what she'd only recently come to accept as the truth. It had taken her a decade of sorting out her feelings to understand it.

"You don't look so good, sis." Jewel would be a great physical therapist. Her empathy didn't quit.

"I'm fine. It's getting hotter in here, isn't it?"

Jewel and Jenna looked at each other, then at Claire.

"We're not hot."

Claire ran a shaky hand through her hair. If they knew about her current attraction to Dutch they'd have her married and living a fairy-tale life.

The thought of spending the rest of her life with him wasn't something she could afford to entertain.

"Well, *I'm* hot. I need to get back to the farm. Sasha's coming over in a few hours. Thanks for making lunch, Jewel."

"No problem. You can do it next week."

"You bet."

Claire got out of the house and slipped behind the wheel of her hybrid compact. It was her running-about-town car. She had a previously owned, beaten-up pickup at the farm that she used for hauling supplies.

She was grateful she'd parked some distance from the house so the twins wouldn't see her slumped back in her seat, head pressed against the neck rest. The discussion about Dutch and their history reverberated through her mind.

She turned the key in the ignition and blasted the air-conditioning, even though the thermometer said it was a mild seventy degrees Fahrenheit.

Guilt clawed at her. The twins were right; everything that had happened between her and Dutch was ancient history.

Yet she'd never swallowed her pride or looked past

her constant attraction to Dutch to reach out to Natalie. After she'd served as maid of honor, she'd given up her acting career.

Because every time she'd been with Natalie and Dutch, she'd had to pretend she was fine, happy in her own life.

And not going crazy with her unrequited love for Dutch and her emotional betrayal of Natalie.

She shoved the gearshift into Drive and left her parents' circular driveway. Memories of that last spring in Dovetail, before college, washed over her. She'd played the victim so well when she'd returned from her weekend away and found out about Dutch and Natalie.

One memory remained intact no matter how many years had gone by. She'd ignored it for so long, but the hurt ran deep. The self-recriminations hadn't gone away.

It was the memory of how she'd let Dutch go first, before his night with Natalie. She'd backed off from him that last semester of high school. She'd felt he was too possessive, too needy, and he didn't want to even talk about her college plans. She didn't understand why he wasn't equally excited about her decision to go far away to college. He was brilliant and could've gone anywhere. But when he was accepted by a college close enough to commute back to Dovetail on the weekends, he'd jumped at it.

Yes, she'd let the relationship go. When she went on an overnight trip her senior year, she and Dutch had all but broken up.

By the time Dutch got together with Natalie the

weekend Claire was out of town, his only attachment to her was one of habit. They'd been together so long, grown up side by side, that they'd left things as they were. No big fight, no messy breakup.

Until Dutch had wound up in Natalie's arms, Natalie in his. It was almost a natural evolution; they were all changing so much, so quickly, back then. And Tom's fatal accident had pushed Dutch and Natalie over the edge, to each other.

All the justification, all the rationales in the world, hadn't kept the truth from devastating Claire when she came back that weekend. Dutch and Natalie had sat down with her and they'd faced one another in complete honesty. Natalie couldn't hide anything from her best friend, and Dutch would rather Claire found out from them than from gossip or rumors.

Claire knew the story by heart. Intellectually she understood what had happened. Much of it hadn't been personal, just part of a tough year in high school.

But Claire had still ended up with a broken heart.

A heart she'd come back to Dovetail to mend. She turned into her driveway and paused in front of the cottage that came with her property. She was going to use it as a shop, a place to sell her llama fiber. Like the farmhouse, the barn and this cottage, building her heart wasn't going to happen without a lot of hard work.

CHAPTER SIX

DUTCH GRITTED his teeth as Sasha went on and on about Claire, still excited about their visits to the llama farm that had happened almost a week ago.

"She's nice, Daddy. I don't see why you're so upset about me wanting to go back to see Claire."

"You're too busy with school, dance and 4-H. And did I mention your dad has a job to do, as well?"

Sasha shot him one of her knowing smiles. When had she started doing that—making adult expressions with her child's face?

"I could get a ride from Aunt Ginny, or you could drop me off. Claire said she'd help me with my 4-H project if I want to do it with the crias or about llamas."

"Let's keep the focus on getting your math home-work done and dinner on the table, okay? Besides, we have to get used to not having Aunt Ginny around. You're losing your chauffeur, kid."

"Humph." Sasha turned back to her open math book while Dutch stirred the spaghetti sauce he'd pulled from the freezer.

Dutch recognized her posture, her attitude. It had been Natalie's whenever she felt she knew more about something than Dutch did.

"Dad!" Sasha's concentration on her figures had lasted all of ten seconds. "You can sign a permission slip for me to get off the bus at the last stop—it's at the bottom of Claire's drive. The bus goes right by it every morning. *And* every afternoon on the way back to the bus depot."

She wasn't giving him any wiggle room.

"We'll talk about it later, Sasha. Besides, Claire's really busy with the llamas and trying to get her farm up and running." He frowned. "She didn't outright invite you, did she?"

"Of *course* she did, Dad." Sasha's impatience shone from her eyes. "You know she'd love to have me out there." Sasha looked down, pouting. "Besides, she was a friend of Mom's. I like hearing about Mom."

Crap.

He knew he shouldn't have brought Sasha after that first visit. It only gave her and Claire time to talk. From the snippets he'd caught, most of the conversation revolved around Natalie as a child.

He sighed and added some basil to the tomato sauce. It wasn't the conversation that irked him; it was the fact that Sasha had already bonded with Claire. Just like that.

Dutch put down the spoon and covered the pot of sauce. He made sure the flame was as low as he could get it before he slid onto the stool next to Sasha. He turned her toward him and held her hands.

"I know you miss Mom, honey. You realize you can ask me or Aunt Ginny anything you want to about her, right?"

"Of course I do, Dad. But you have to admit, neither you or Aunt Ginny was as close to Mom as Claire was, not when you were little or even my age."

Dutch looked into eyes as brown as Natalie's had been. When did his little girl become such a young woman?

"No. You're right about that." He'd known Claire forever—hell, they'd started with wooden blocks and had gone through video games, computer games, you name it, together. His interest in Natalie had come later, when it was obvious Claire had her sights set on anything but Dovetail. Or him.

Claire, however, had been part of Natalie's life forever.

Dutch kissed Sasha's forehead.

"You can go with me next time, but please promise me that you won't get your hopes up too much. Claire's never had her own kids, and she doesn't have to cater to us, okay?"

"Dad, I'm not going to force you guys to be friends or anything. I get it." Her posture of maturity almost fooled him.

"Great." He stood and went back to the spaghetti sauce.

He knew Sasha didn't *really* get it. Sasha didn't want him to think she was playing matchmaker, but he saw the warning signs. She had no idea that he and Claire hadn't needed a matchmaker once upon a time.

His mind's eye glimpsed an old image. Claire on an azure beach towel, her golden skin covered only by her bright orange bikini.

His hand shook as he dipped the wooden spoon into the sauce, and it wasn't from hunger. Neither was the perspiration that gathered on the back of his neck.

CLAIRE STOOD on the stepladder and reached her dust mop to the top edge of the cottage wall. A little bit of oil soap and a lot of work was making the old place downright homey.

She loved the smell of the cleaning potions as they washed away the dust and the musty odor of decades of disuse. The previous owners had used the cottage as a guesthouse, until they grew old and the friends who once visited passed on.

Claire only knew about the cottage and the history of her farmhouse because she'd grown up in Dovetail. She made a mental note to go to the state archives at some point and make sure she'd gathered all the information available on this property. There was bound to be a good marketing angle in the history.

As she cleaned, moving from wall to wall in the tiny house, she envisioned the shelves where she'd put bins of yarn. The counter with the cash register could go closer to the front door. It wasn't going to be a huge store, but big enough to draw people in and provide education about llamas and llama fiber. Maybe she'd even have a few alpacas in the next year or two.

"Don't get ahead of yourself. Become an expert on llamas first." She spoke to the cobwebs her mop collected in a corner.

"Do you always talk to yourself when you work?"

Dutch's voice carried up to her ears at the same moment she felt his hands on her ankles.

"I was afraid I'd startle you," he explained.

She took in a deep breath and regarded him from her perch. She clung to the mop so he wouldn't see her hands shaking. The warmth of his fingers on her ankles provided more than a steadying factor. Bolts of excitement shot up her legs and warmed her belly.

And it was only half past nine in the morning.

"You did—I'm surprised I didn't hear you with the door open." She'd left the front door ajar to catch the fresh breeze blowing across the fields.

"You were obviously in another place." The lines around Dutch's eyes and mouth deepened. Was that actually a smile on his face? In her presence?

"Here, let me help you down."

Before she had a chance to do anything else, Dutch grasped her by the waist and lifted her onto the cottage's wide-planked floor. She looked at him.

"I suppose lifting animals all day makes that easier for you, but you could've given yourself a hernia."

He laughed. Claire maintained her neutral expression, but knew her eyes reflected her chagrin.

"Trust me. I've carried calves and crias heavier than you."

Yeah, right.

She kept the thought to herself. The awareness between them grabbed hold of Claire's heart and she tried to catch her breath.

"Is something wrong with Nip or Tuck? Or Stormy?"

"Hmm?" Dutch was staring at her face and, more pointedly, her lips.

She took a step back. Dutch got the hint and the light in his eyes dimmed. He was back to business.

"The llamas—are they okay?" She repeated her query as a way of creating space between them.

"I haven't checked them since this morning, but I'm sure they're fine. I think it's safe to say we can go to once-a-day, even every-other-day, checks."

Relief and gratitude lifted the invisible weight from Claire's shoulders. "They're doing that well?"

"Yes, they are."

"I can never thank you enough for all you've done, Dutch. If you'd come a few minutes later…"

"But I didn't, and you were there, doing whatever you could. It's my job, Claire." He brushed off her thanks. He was in a better mood than she'd seen since moving back, and certainly since he'd been tending to the llamas.

"Is that why you came in here, to tell me the llamas don't need as much vet care?"

"No, actually, I have a favor to ask."

This was interesting. Dutch, asking *her* for a favor?

"Okay. Shoot." She leaned the mop against the wall and shoved her hands in her jeans pockets.

"Sasha really wants to spend more time out here with the llamas."

"With the llamas?"

"Yes, and well…with you." His reluctance hurt a little.

"That's perfectly fine, Dutch. You don't need to ask me as a favor—it's my honor to spend time with Natalie's daughter. And yours." She hastily added that when she realized how sharp her reply sounded.

Dutch held up a hand.

"It's not just about the llamas, Claire." Dutch looked somewhere past her shoulder, then back into her eyes.

His discomfort was palpable. "Sasha's thrilled that you knew Natalie so well as a kid. Let's face it, I didn't really come into Natalie's life—except as a friend—until the end of high school."

Claire prided herself on not wincing. "And?"

Dutch cast her a bemused expression. "You're not going to make this easy for me, are you?" He grimaced. "Hell, why should you?"

He ran his hand across the back of his neck. "As much as I have my reservations about all of this, I realize it's a good thing for Sasha to have relationships with other adults. For her to trust an adult other than family. And you *did* know Natalie at her age, so you can fill in a lot of details for her."

"Dutch, Sasha is welcome here anytime. You don't have to ask me about it again. You and I—" Her breath caught on the last word, then she cleared her throat. "You and I don't need to rehash the past or even talk to each other very much. You can drop her off, or I'll come and get her, and we can hang out here. She already told me the last time you were both here that she's interested in doing her 4-H project with the llamas."

Dutch's face was relaxed again.

"Thanks for understanding." Although his voice was gruff she sensed he was sincere.

"Sasha said she can get off the bus near your place, if that's okay with you. I'll pick her up an hour or so later. I'm thinking maybe once a week." He was hesitant, as if he was asking her for a date.

"By the way, this is entirely Sasha's idea, Claire."

"And you do anything you can for your daughter."

She looked at his lips as she spoke. They were tightly pressed together.

"This is for Sasha," he muttered.

"I get it, Dutch. Don't worry, you haven't given me the wrong impression." He'd never let up on reminding her of his distrust.

She took a deep breath and raised her chin. She met his gaze and kept her voice steady. "Why don't we decide on two days a week so it's a regular part of her schedule? If you're tied up with work, I'll run her home or she can wait for you here. I rarely go out in the evenings."

Darn it! Not something she wanted Dutch to know. The last thing she needed was for him to think she was pining away for lack of a love life.

You don't *have a love life.*

"And if I have an evening date I can let you know ahead of time." There. Let him chew on that.

"I'm sure you will." Dutch looked as if he was going to turn away, but he paused. "Claire, I want it clear between you and me that there *is* no 'you and me.' I'd appreciate it if you didn't lead Sasha to assume anything different."

Heat rushed into her cheeks.

What the heck had she thought, making that comment about a "date"? She sounded as though she was out on the prowl. Way to reinforce Dutch's low opinion of her morals.

"That's all in the past, Dutch."

"Yes, but Sasha doesn't know you as anyone other than her mother's childhood friend. She doesn't need to know any more. Nor do I want her to get any silly ideas that'll only break her heart later on."

"I got it," she said again.

With that he pivoted and walked out of the cottage.

Claire wanted to throw the mop at him. Or better yet, the bucket of soapy water. Typical Dutch—come in all charming and then leave her feeling like a complete loser.

She grabbed the mop and went back to her cleaning. If she focused on her desire to make amends to Natalie for abandoning their friendship, she'd be fine. She'd be here for Sasha, regardless of her relationship with Dutch.

The problem was that whenever Dutch was around she couldn't keep her eyes off him. Her hands itched to touch him. And a few minutes earlier she'd thought he was going to kiss her. And she would've kissed him back—hard.

Don't lose sight of your goal. She'd finally rebuilt her reputation in Dovetail and even Dutch would acknowledge that she ran a decent llama farm.

A romance with him was not a possibility.

"DECAF?"

"Sure. You got any of that Easter cake left?" Dutch smiled at Dottie as she poured his coffee.

"Let me check. We ran out last night, but Mel was supposed to have another one ready by lunchtime." Dottie frowned, the coffeepot held in one hand. "You're not getting lunch first?"

"Nope. I have three farms to visit before Sasha gets off the bus."

"You can't survive on sweets, Dutch."

"Aw, Dottie, I don't do this that often."

"True." She eyed him. "Only when you're upset. What's got you going this time? Or should I say *who?*"

Dutch jerked on his stool, as if Dottie's slap had been physical.

"No one's got me going, Dot." He threw back half the coffee and groaned.

"Burned your mouth, did you?" Dottie smiled and sauntered off to serve a new customer.

Dottie was right, but he'd never admit it, not to her. Yeah, he was definitely stirred up. By Claire Renquist.

He'd acted like a teenager. His brain had gone straight to his crotch the minute he saw her on the stepladder in her tight jeans. She was no longer a girl; she was a woman with a body that didn't quit. It was hard to ignore her sexiness, despite the dumpy sweaters and old jeans she wore.

The chemistry between them had only intensified. He wondered if what he felt today had anything to with how he'd felt about her as a teenager. But this was deeper, stronger.

He'd had his share of dates since Natalie died, and he didn't want for companionship—it was there if he asked for it. But he'd never brought a woman home, never got involved enough to necessitate introducing Sasha to his date. He made sure the women he saw weren't from nearby. The Internet was good for that sort of thing.

He sighed and sipped his coffee. It had cooled, but his desire hadn't. He didn't want another date, a one-night stand to ease his physical needs. He wanted someone he could share his life with. Someone who could be a mother to Sasha.

The realization that it was time to look for more in a woman than an evening's companionship—or a warm bed—suddenly hit him. Coffee sloshed over the side of his mug as he set it down.

Why did it have to be Claire who'd made him aware of his need for a life partner?

He could never be with Claire. Even if he was able to forgive her for hurting Natalie, he'd never shake the feeling that Claire was going to catch the next train out of here.

"You're thinking way too hard." Dottie slid the porcelain plate with its huge piece of hummingbird cake that Mel, her baker, always made for the spring holidays.

"This will cure it." Dutch grinned and forked up a large bite. He usually didn't give in to his sweet tooth, but every now and then it was worth it.

"Mel has the touch, that's for sure." As if hearing her own words, Dottie's hands stilled and her face flushed.

"Dottie, do you have a thing for your baker?" Dutch teased.

"Me? You've got to be kidding! I've been widowed for over ten years. Why do I need a man in my life now?"

"Why not?" He didn't point out that she'd avoided the question.

"Because I'm happy on my own, that's why." She stared at him. "What about you, Dutch? You and Sasha could use someone—for both of you."

"When the time's right." He swallowed some coffee with the last bite of cake. "And when it's the right person."

Dottie watched him wolf down the last of the cake. "Sometimes the right person isn't of your choosing, Dutch. And don't expect her to show up on your time line, either. Life has a way of giving us what we need rather than what we want."

Before he could respond, she added, "Or what we *think* we want."

CHAPTER SEVEN

THE NEXT DAY, Dutch and Sasha pulled into Claire's driveway at four-fifteen. He immediately swerved to miss the person walking in the middle of the drive.

He stopped and lowered his window.

Claire's eyes were wide. "I thought Sasha was coming on the bus—hi, Sasha!" She waved at the girl who bounced in the front passenger seat. So Claire had intended to meet Sasha at the end of the drive, right where the bus would have dropped her.

Well, that was *one* point for Claire. She showed the same protectiveness toward Sasha that he did.

"Hi, Claire!" Sasha screamed her greeting in Dutch's ear. He turned and looked at his daughter, the only reason he was back at Claire's place. After coming dangerously close to blowing his resolve about keeping his distance from Claire, he would've preferred to visit the llamas when Claire wasn't around.

Yeah, right.

"I'm getting out—wait!" Sasha yelled to Claire, again through Dutch's head.

"Would you mind sparing your dad's hearing, Sash?"

She giggled. "Sorry, Dad." Then she asked, "Can I get out and walk with Claire?"

"Sure. I'll bring your bag up to the house."

"Thanks." Sasha slid out of the cab and slammed the door behind her. He waited for her to clear the hood and start walking alongside Claire.

Sasha reached up and grabbed the knit cap off Claire's head. He didn't recognize the emotion that clenched his gut. What did Sasha see in Claire?

He groaned. Was he actually jealous of Claire—and Sasha's growing adoration of her?

He felt as low as a toad in a ditch. Sasha was his daughter, and he was doing this for her sake. He didn't need to feel envious of anyone else's relationship with her, at least not until she brought home her first boyfriend.

Still…Dutch didn't like how this was going. Claire and Sasha bent toward each other as they examined Claire's hat. It was a pretty miserable attempt at a hat; even he could tell that.

Yet Sasha's hands were near Claire's, feeling the stitches Claire had knit. As if she'd known Claire her whole life. As if Claire had never hurt her father or her mother.

In his mind he saw Claire's hand holding a crochet hook when they were juniors in high school. Her hand— hell, all of her—had mesmerized him back then. He clearly remembered her working with the bright blue yarn that was their school's color. He'd thought Claire was making herself something to wear to the Dovetail Dogs games, but she'd given it to him at Christmas—a scarf.

That was a long time ago, man.

He shook the memory off.

Stopping the truck, he waited for them to catch up,

then leaned out the window. Rascal, who'd come along for the ride, poked his head out alongside Dutch.

"Sasha, I'm sure Claire has work to get done. Why don't you sit in the truck while I examine the llamas?"

"Dad." Sasha gave him a "what, are you nuts?" look, not unlike Natalie used to.

"Sasha." His voice came out firmer than he'd meant, but it didn't appear to faze Sasha.

"I don't want to get back in the truck, Dad. I'm here to see Claire and the llamas, remember? Plus, I'm helping Claire with her knitting."

"It's fine with me, Dutch." Claire didn't meet his eyes, gazing down at her hat instead. Her tone was neutral for Sasha's sake, but he caught her innuendo. He'd been the one who'd asked to bring Sasha out here; now he was acting like…like some kind of psycho.

Dutch nodded, rolled up the window and drove past them toward the barn. He'd lived long enough to know that a wise man didn't argue with two women at once.

Anger roiled deep in his gut. Who the hell did Claire think she was, saying, "It's fine with me," as if she had a role in any kind of decision-making where his daughter was concerned?

You came here, he told himself. *You allowed Sasha to spend time with her. Move on, man.*

They said raising kids was tough. He realized growing up wasn't easy for Sasha, either. But right now he felt as though *he* was the one with growing pains.

GO STICK YOURSELF in the mud, Claire thought as she watched Dutch slowly drive away. It wasn't like she had some communicable disease, for heaven's sake. And she was the last person who'd ever do anything to hurt Sasha, the daughter of her dearest childhood friend.

"Tell you what, Sash. It's cold out here and your dad's going to be a while. Why don't we go inside and stay warm? You can see the llamas before you leave."

"Great!" Sasha trotted next to Claire. When they passed the barn, Claire glanced over to see Dutch standing next to Stormy, who'd been out in the field all day. She was definitely getting stronger.

He looked up, and Claire turned back to Sasha. They'd reached the gravel path to the house's side steps.

"Careful, these are tricky. I plan to rip them out and extend the front porch to a wraparound as soon as I can afford to."

Sasha gave the farmhouse an assessing glance.

"I think a big porch would be cool. Will you screen it in? Our back deck isn't screened and we can never sit out there in the summer. The mosquitoes are terrible!"

Claire laughed. "I hadn't thought that far ahead, but you're right—no sense having a nice porch if you can't enjoy it. I'll have to add screening to my budget."

As soon as she started making some serious money from the farm. If it wasn't for her freelance consulting work, she couldn't afford to continue living here and running the farm.

Claire opened the door and ushered Sasha into the kitchen.

"But didn't your reporter job make you rich?" As she spoke Sasha's eyes moved from side to side, taking in every detail.

Claire pulled out a heavy oak chair from the farm table she'd found on consignment last summer. "Hardly. I mean, I had a bit of a nest egg that enabled me to buy the house and farm and the first few llamas." In fact, she'd barely covered the costs of the past year with the beginnings of her llama fiber business. If she hadn't met a woman willing to hand-spin some of the fiber so Claire could sell it out of the barn, her finances would've been quite dismal.

"So how do you make money?"

"I'm still working as an independent contractor for various government agencies. They ask for my opinion on different issues, and I write a report." She took out the ingredients for hot chocolate and two mugs. Then she added a third mug; Dutch was bound to be chilled when he came in from the barn.

"Eventually, I hope to have a full stock, everything from roving—" she referred to the raw fiber product "—to yarn, in all colors. I'll sell all kinds of fibers, from suppliers all over the world, but the only llama fiber I want to sell is mine."

Sasha nodded thoughtfully.

"I think a llama blend is best, and I'd like to have different types for sale," Claire explained. "Llama's the most successful when it's blended with other fibers that hold their shape better—like soy, silk or merino. I might also invest in alpacas."

"Alpacas are neat. I saw one at the state fair last year."

Claire agreed. The smaller, gentler version of the llama also produced a finer fiber, one that sold at more lucrative prices.

"Yeah, well, it all takes time." Claire measured the

cocoa powder into their mugs while they waited for the kettle to whistle.

"Did you notice that small building closer to the road when you came in?" she asked.

"The haunted cottage?"

Claire raised her eyebrows. "It's haunted?"

"We drive by it on our school bus in the afternoon, and everyone says it's been haunted since forever."

"Really?" Claire smiled at how the building seemed so old to the young kids. It hadn't seemed that old when she, Dutch and Natalie were kids.

"The daughter of the owner before me tried to turn it into a B and B." At Sasha's blank look, Claire explained, "Bed and breakfast."

Claire stirred the hot chocolate as she poured hot water over it. "But they got ill before they could realize their dream. It was never even remodeled. I'm turning the cottage into a yarn shop."

"Cool."

Based on her expectant look, Sasha seemed happy just to be in a conversation with her, even if talk of Claire's business bored her.

She decided to change the subject. "What's your favorite subject in school?"

Sasha tilted her head. "I like Social Studies, especially when we learn about a really different country. But I really love Earth Science. I love stuff about the planets and space."

"Hmm. You could become a meteorologist."

"Yeah, but the math part isn't so fun. I mean, math's easy for me, but kind of dull, you know?"

Claire couldn't imagine anything Sasha didn't excel at. The bright intelligence in her gaze was familiar. Dutch had held the number-one spot in their high school class all four years.

Dutch.

Claire ignored the voice that told her she was crazy for going anywhere near Dutch or Sasha.

She'd been Natalie's best friend for most of their lives—at least until Dutch had connected with Natalie. Claire could share her early history with Sasha, fill in some details about her mother....

"What did my mom want to be when she was my age? Do you remember?"

"Let me think." Claire blew on her hot chocolate. "When we were younger, in third or fourth grade, she wanted to be a nurse. She'd read about Florence Nightingale in Social Studies and because she liked the smell of brand-new Band-Aids she figured it was the job for her. Then she read *Nancy Drew*—"

"And wanted to be a detective?" Sasha obviously knew Carolyn Keene's heroine.

"Yes, of course!" When Claire laughed, Sasha let out a giggle, and they exchanged a glance that reminded Claire of the joie de vivre she and Natalie had shared for their entire childhood. Until Tom's death. And Dutch's betrayal.

Claire's laughter died. Until recently, she'd blamed Dutch for their breakup. But they'd been kids, teenagers, and she'd been so focused on getting out of Dovetail... Maybe she'd played a bigger part than she'd realized.

Maybe you never forgave Natalie for not under-standing your *pain.*

That sudden insight brought a stab of guilt.

Sasha stared at her. Could she read Claire's mind?

"Why don't we knit for a while? Did you bring yours?"

Sasha hauled her backpack onto her lap. "Yeah, I've got a scarf I'm making for my friend Maddie."

They each put down their hot chocolate and started to knit. Claire admired how natural it was for Sasha. The needles still felt rather foreign in her own hands, espe-cially when she was working on a new stitch.

"Claire?"

"Hmm?" Claire looked up from her knitting.

Sasha had a somberness in her eyes that Claire sus-pected she'd better get used to. It always preceded a doozy of a question.

"Why didn't you ever come to see my mother?"

Claire's hand jerked and she lost her stitch. The lush wool fell from her fingers.

She took a deep breath and lowered her hands to her lap, forcing them to be still. Sasha deserved her com-plete attention.

"It's not that I didn't want to. It just…got too diffi-cult. Between my job, your mom's job and family life, it was almost impossible to schedule any visits. Your mom didn't have time to come into D.C. very much, and I couldn't take time off to drive out here."

Claire knew she owed Sasha more than such an am-biguous reply. "Sometimes adults let distractions get in the way of doing what's right," she finally said.

"What kind of distractions did you have?" Looking into Sasha's brown eyes, Claire felt as if she'd been convicted. She tried to explain, anyway.

"Well, I was working in the press corps—the group of reporters who follow the president all over the world. We were in the midst of one crisis after another, and I had to stay on top of every story."

"But weren't you one of lots of people who reported about the president?"

"Yes, I was one of many reporters, actually. But everyone thinks they're the most valuable—that the story won't get told properly without them. I believed that, just like everyone else, I'm afraid."

"You never got a day off?"

"Not really." She looked at Sasha and wondered what was going on behind that clear, open gaze. "But that's not the point, Sasha. I realize now that I could have, *should* have, made time to see your mom, especially when she was sick. My last visit, you were in full-day school already. Before that, I hadn't seen you since you were an infant."

Claire remembered Natalie's baby shower all too clearly. The baby, Sasha, had arrived two weeks early and so the shower had taken place after the birth instead of the week before.

It had been a nightmare for Claire. She'd been the only unmarried woman there—and the only one without a baby in her near future. Seeing Dutch and Natalie's baby had been excruciating. She'd thought back then that she simply didn't relate to the whole baby thing, but today she realized it was more than that.

She hadn't wanted to see that Dutch and Natalie were truly happy together. That their love had created a tiny human being.

"I don't remember you, except from TV."

Ouch.

"There's no reason you would—you were a newborn when I first met you and, as I said, in school during that last visit. Your parents might not have even mentioned that I'd stopped by."

Claire would never admit it to Sasha, but she'd planned that trip for late morning, when she knew Dutch would be at work and Sasha in school. Natalie on her own she could handle.

When it was just the two of them, she could pretend that their friendship had survived the years and Claire's broken heart.

Claire had never told Natalie about her sense of betrayal or her unrequited feelings for Dutch. Part of it was Claire's unwillingness to hurt others. A bigger part of it was pride. She'd never told anyone that Dutch had broken her heart.

Including Natalie.

Claire knew she had to examine her resentment against Natalie. How could Natalie have sympathized with Claire if Claire hadn't told her how hurt she was over her marriage to Dutch? And yet…Claire had come to understand that she bore some responsibility for what had happened. After high school she'd let her relationship with Dutch grow stale, diminish in importance. And she'd let her friendship with Natalie die away.

"I loved your mom like a sister the entire time we

were growing up. As adults our lives took different paths. Like I said, it wasn't only me not coming home, your mom never made it into D.C., either."

In truth, Natalie had come to Georgetown once, before she got sick; and stayed with Claire overnight. Claire gave her a tour of the White House and Natalie sat through a press conference.

After which Natalie, in true brute-honest Natalie fashion, had told Claire she needed to have more in her life than work.

Claire had been a press corps reporter for two years already, and Natalie made it clear that she thought Claire had been ignoring her social life, that she lacked balance.

Claire hadn't wanted to hear Natalie's opinion, no matter how sensible. But instead of arguing, she'd used it as an excuse to further distance herself from her friend. Natalie had assumed Claire was angry at her for what she had said, and Claire never corrected the assumption. She thought it was easier for both of them if she dropped the relationship.

"I spoke to your dad after your mom's last chemo." The one they'd all prayed would allow her to pull through, protect her from the last stages of her disease. But it hadn't.

"I'm sorry, Sasha. I should've come back to see your mom, to meet you. I had every intention of coming. But I missed my chance by a week. I had an emergency trip with the president that my network needed me to cover."

And after that, it was too late. She couldn't, wouldn't, intrude on the family's grief.

"Dying, like having a baby, is intensely private. I didn't want to take anything away from your mom's time with you and your dad."

"Hmm." Sasha's ponytail swished as she nodded.

Claire hoped "hmm" meant that Sasha's inquisition was over.

Claire picked up the wool she'd dropped and stuck the needles into the ball.

"Would you like a refill on your hot chocolate? I've finished mine."

"I'm okay." Sasha kept knitting and pulled her yarn from a beautiful silk yarn bag. No doubt it had been Natalie's. Claire's throat tightened and she turned her face away.

She had no illusion of replacing Natalie in Sasha's life. But she wanted to somehow make up for her own transgressions against Natalie. She hadn't realized it was going to be this difficult. She hadn't understood the depth of her own grief at Natalie's loss.

Fingers rapped on the glass panes of the side door and Claire opened it.

Dutch's eyes flashed in obvious anger. "Time to go, Sasha." He remained on the top step, ignoring Claire.

"Claire's making me another hot chocolate." Sasha had apparently developed a convenient thirst.

Dutch's lips thinned and his face grew impassive.

"Why don't you come in for a minute, Dutch? It's cold, and you're letting all the heat out."

He didn't reply as he stepped inside the kitchen and shut the door behind him. His stance conveyed his wariness of Claire.

"Don't act like a cornered mouse, Dutch." She spoke in a low voice. "You're safe here."

Dutch grunted. Claire wanted to smack him, but instead poured hot water into a mug and mixed in more cocoa powder.

"How are my llamas?" she asked.

Dutch blew out a breath and shoved his clenched hands in the front pockets of his jeans. Claire hated herself for permitting her gaze to follow his hands and linger over the area between his pockets. He'd filled out since their late teens and become more rugged.

Sexier.

Claire looked away, but not soon enough. Dutch's eyes narrowed, and she knew that if Sasha hadn't been in the room he'd have a few choice words about keeping her distance.

She shoved the mug at him. "Here. This'll warm you up."

He pulled his hands out of his pockets and took the mug before she spilled its contents all over his chest. One eyebrow rose, indicating that even he saw a hint of humor in the situation.

"Your llamas? They're doing well. The weather should help when it decides to warm up, but they're fine."

"Thank goodness," she murmured. "It's been so cold. I don't remember a March or April this cold when we were kids."

The childhood memory produced a moment's awkward silence.

"Would you like something to eat?" She'd found her manners again.

"No, thanks. We need to leave as soon as we finish this." He downed the rest of his cocoa. "Sasha?"

Sasha's eyelids were lowered as she held her fresh cup of hot cocoa. Claire knew the kid hadn't missed a single note of the conversation. What did she make of Claire and Dutch? The blatantly rude way they addressed each other?

Sasha threw back her head and drained the mug.

She stood. "Thanks, Claire. I had a nice time."

"Me, too."

Sasha stood there expectantly, watching Claire. Claire looked back at her, dumbfounded. What was it?

"Okay, well, bye." Sasha walked over and stood in front of Claire.

Oh...

"See you around." Claire gave Sasha the hug she'd been waiting for, all the while conscious of Dutch's perturbed glare.

Sasha passed her dad and ran down the steps.

"Cozy." Dutch issued the one-word observation like a missile.

"You've raised a daughter who's used to lots of love and support. That's commendable."

Dutch sent Claire another hard gaze—and then she saw his stony expression dissolve.

"She *has* had that. It's important to me that she not get hurt. She craves female adult attention and I hope you realize what a trusting young girl she is."

Claire appreciated his honesty, and was stunned that he'd opened up even this much. But she didn't need another reminder of the gap Natalie's death had left in all their lives.

"Of course." She cleared her throat. "Thanks for checking on the animals."

"It's my job. I'll be back in a few days. Call me if you need me sooner." Dutch turned on the porch, his foot raised to go down the steps, then turned back.

"You've done an admirable job with the llamas."

She watched him descend the steps before she closed the door and leaned against it. Not until she heard the pickup's engine, did she respond.

"Thank you."

CHAPTER EIGHT

"CALL ME WHEN you get in." Dutch knew Ginny didn't like being treated like his kid sister. But she *was* his kid sister.

"Sure." Ginny put the last of her books in the back of her small sedan. She straightened up and shut the door. They'd both known this day would come. And with Ginny's commitment to the law preparatory class, it had arrived a few months earlier than he'd hoped.

"You be good." She patted his upper arm. "Dutch? Try to keep an open mind."

"About what?" His sister always had an uncanny sense of his emotional state.

"About everything. Natalie's been gone for over three years, and she never wanted you to be a monk."

"Why do I think you're talking about Claire?"

"Claire?" Ginny opened her eyes wide in pretended innocence. But Dutch knew damn well that his little sister wasn't naive on this subject at all.

"Well, now that you mention it, Sasha needs a woman in her life. Since I'm leaving, it *is* rather fortuitous that Claire's around. And that she knew Natalie as a kid. They were really close, Dutch."

"Don't even *try* to guilt me into this, Ginny."

Ginny's signature laugh-with-a-snort coaxed his lips up in spite of his exasperation with his sister. Her dark corkscrew curls bobbed about her face.

"Any guilt you have is because you know it's the truth. You're entitled to your opinion of Claire, Dutch, but she's a good person underneath it all. Don't deny Sasha a connection to Natalie because of your own selfishness."

Dutch opened his mouth to blast Ginny, then snapped it shut. He wasn't going to win this one, and besides, he didn't want to send Ginny away in a bad mood.

"Give me a hug, bro."

Ginny hugged him tight and he hugged her back.

"I can't thank you enough, Gin."

"Shh, don't be silly. It helped all of us. It's time for me to get my degree, and for you and Sasha to get your own life."

Tears burned his eyes as he hugged his sister. She'd been such a rock for all of them.

Ginny pulled away. "Knock it off, Dutch. You need to get dinner going if you want to eat tonight."

"Yeah." He stood there as she walked around her car and slid into the driver's seat. After a few adjustments, she backed down their drive, shifted gears and headed for Baltimore.

Ginny would be fine; he knew it. And God help who-ever crossed her in a courtroom.

Yeah, Ginny would be okay. And Sasha would, too; he'd make sure of it.

But would he?

CLAIRE ENTERED the bookstore, where the knitting group was in session. The previous time she'd tried to join them, she'd been unprepared, but today her basket held several balls of yarn, several varieties and sizes of needles and three different projects she'd started.

Today she knew that this used to be Natalie's group, and when she'd first shown up the women present couldn't help but connect her to her childhood friend.

Plus, she had her wits about her now. Wits weren't something she'd had a lot of immediately after she'd left the press corps. Until the doctors had determined the extent of her mother's illness and Claire got used to small-town living again, she'd been in a whirl of change.

Then it'd taken her a while to adjust to the idea that her mother was fine, and her dad could take care of her very well, thank you. They didn't need Claire over there each and every day. And she had to face the fact that she hadn't come home for Mom, not really. She'd come back to find herself again. Mom's illness had only precipitated a quicker move.

Mrs. Ames looked up, her black-penciled eyebrows in sharp contrast to her snowy mane of shoulder-length hair and her crystal-blue irises.

"Oh, you're back?" Mrs. Ames spoke as if Claire had been there last week and not nearly a year ago.

"Of course! Where is everyone?"

"Group starts at ten-thirty. You're early."

Mrs. Ames returned to her knitting—a gauzy length that Claire surmised was a lace stole or shawl.

"That's lovely." She pointed at the other woman's

work. "What are you making?" Claire knew good manners would carry her further than an antagonistic attitude, warranted or not.

"A prayer shawl for my church ministry."

Claire slid into the seat across from her. "That's a wonderful idea! Do you think I could learn to make one?"

"Of course." Mrs. Ames peered into the basket Claire placed on the table between them. "Ooh, looks like you've been making progress!" The pleased tone was unexpected.

"I've been learning on the Internet and from a friend. I know I should finish one project before I begin another, but I can't help myself."

"Nonsense. It's important to have several projects going at once. I always do. Keeps me interested. I finish them as needed—whether a gift for me or someone else."

Relief washed over Claire. "I must admit I'm thrilled to hear you say that. I thought I might have some kind of knitting attention-deficit disorder."

Mrs. Ames laughed. "No more than the rest of us— oh, look, here comes Patsy."

Patsy Lovette sashayed in, her giraffe-print jacket an odd mix with her blueberry shade of dyed hair and fuchsia scarf.

"Hey." She cast a curious glance at Claire and bent to air-kiss Mrs. Ames.

"You remember each other, don't you?" Mrs. Ames offered as introduction.

Claire smiled at Patsy. How could they forget? They'd both competed for the same spot on the high school gymnastics team. Claire won in ninth and tenth grade, but Patsy had taken the spot as a junior and senior. They'd never been real enemies, but not close friends, either.

"Hi," Claire said.

"Hi, honey, I heard you were back in town. Didn't know you were a knitter, though." Patsy wasn't at the group that disastrous time the year before.

Claire shoved the memory aside. She'd assumed it would be a group of genteel older ladies all too willing to teach a young woman like her the techniques of their craft. Not the lively women she'd discovered, many of whom still grieved Natalie.

"So what are you working on?" Patsy nodded at Claire's basket.

Claire had faced world leaders with what they perceived as hostile interview questions. She'd stared down prevaricating government officials. She could handle opposition and criticism with the best of them; she knew not to take it personally.

But her knitting projects *were* highly personal. She'd labored over learning the stitches and deciding which patterns she could attempt with her limited skills. Learning to knit was part of how she'd redefined herself.

To her dismay, her hands shook as she reached into her basket. She yanked up the first project she touched, hoping that her action covered her nervousness.

"This is a scarf and this—" she pulled out a brown square "—is the first of thirty-six squares for an afghan I saw in a magazine."

Patsy's hands were all over her projects, caressing the yarn. "Oooh, is this alpaca?"

"No, it's a blend of llama and merino."

"Really? Did you buy that around here?"

"She's probably one of those Internet yarn buyers, aren't you, Claire? Your generation doesn't go to stores as much." Mrs. Ames sniffed and kept up with her knitting, using the plastic needles Claire had tried, but found uncomfortable in her hands.

"Actually, it's from the farm where I bought my llamas." Claire felt a certain smugness—she might not knit well, but she'd learned a great deal about fiber over the past couple of years. "Llama fiber tends to stretch, so even though it's warm and soft like alpaca, it works best when it's spun with another wool or natural fiber."

Patsy nodded again. "You're really gonna make a go of this—your llama farm?"

Claire couldn't keep the smile off her face. "That's my plan."

"Give me a high five!" Claire hesitated when Patsy held up a slim, acrylic-nailed hand, but then raised her own worn, short-nailed hand and landed a firm smack on Patsy's palm.

"Now *this* is what I'm talking about, Claire. Women need to do their own thing and show the world we can do it."

"Sure." Claire smiled. She and Patsy would never share fashion taste nor be close friends, but they had a common history.

And now they had knitting.

Claire settled in and started knitting her second

square for the afghan. She watched as each woman appeared, and then, to her surprise, a man joined the group. Tall, elegant and with a shock of white hair, Mr. Black had been Claire's tenth-grade English teacher. She'd loved that class. She also remembered the unending teasing Mr. Black had taken. Not directly to his face, but the guys in class made jokes about his sexual preference, often within his earshot. The girls usually frowned, not sure why their male classmates cared if Mr. Black was gay or not.

"Hey, Donald." A chorus of female voices greeted their lone male.

"Good morning, ladies." He smiled at each woman. His gaze rested on Claire's for a moment.

"Claire Renquist. Row two, three from the window." His voice hadn't changed. It was still the same deep melodious voice that had read passages of Shakespeare to them as they struggled to grasp the meaning.

Claire wanted to hug Mr. Black, but didn't know the ins and outs of knit-group etiquette. "So nice to see you again, Mr. Black."

Mr. Black folded his frame into the single chair left in the circle. He pulled an intricate Scandinavian-looking sweater from his bag and started knitting. Claire observed the deftness of his long-fingered hands and the casual manner with which he wove two colors into such a detailed pattern.

He raised his dark eyes and caught her stare. "I never did reveal my love of knitting to my English Lit classes." The whole group laughed, and Claire marveled at this softer, friendlier version of Mr. Black. He'd been an erudite teacher, his passion for story evident, but he'd never revealed an inkling of his personal life to the students.

"No, but you taught the best class I've ever taken. Even in college my professors didn't have the grasp of story structure and theme that you did, Mr. Black."

"Why, thank you so much, Claire. And please call me Donald. I haven't been Mr. Black for years."

"So you retired?"

"Yes, to write the great American novel, of course. What else do retired English teachers do?"

"They knit!" Mrs. Ames piped up and the group laughed again.

Mr. Black chuckled and pulled up a strand of red yarn. "Yes, I knit."

"Is that sweater for you?"

He gave Claire a measured look over his glasses.

"No, it's for my partner, Jim."

"It's gorgeous. He's very lucky to get it."

"He snagged the other one on barbed wire when he was bringing in hay last fall."

Claire's expression must have revealed her horror. What a beautiful sweater, with so much love knit into it. And his partner had worn it to *harvest?*

"Jim loves the fit and design of all the things Donald's made him, but he doesn't get it when it comes to the quality part, or the time." Patsy filled in some of the blanks.

"He doesn't get the cost of the fiber, either," Donald grumbled, but it was clear from his tone that he'd knit a sweater every month for his partner if he had to.

Claire felt a warm sense of security that she hadn't had in years. She was glad Mr. Black had a good life and someone to love. It was nice to be with him again, this time without adolescent boys making snarky, ignorant remarks. She was also relieved that no one in the knitting group had critiqued her knitting ability.

I'm happy to be here.

After two years of often backbreaking work, Claire felt the tension in her shoulders begin to dissipate. This was where she belonged.

CLAIRE SETTLED into the rhythm of her knitting as the group's chatter waxed and waned. Sometimes two people conversed; sometimes all the knitters took part in a cacophony over a subject that could be simple, like how to cast on stitches for a fine-gauge cardigan. Once the topic was where to find the best mammogram and breast care in the area. And as they talked, they knitted.

The olive-colored yarn moved easily through Claire's fingers as she reached the halfway point on another square for the blanket. She wanted to use it in the farmhouse's cottage-size living area. Maybe one day when the farm was doing well she'd have enough cash to remodel that front room, enlarge it and raise the ceiling. Make it into a great room, combined with the kitchen—what she'd envisioned when she first saw the tired-looking interior.

Claire glanced around the group. Even though they drove from all over to get to this chain bookstore, the majority of the knitters were from Dovetail. This plaza was only about twenty minutes from Claire's driveway, so it was ideal for her. She got a break from Dovetail and the farm, but wasn't so far away that she felt she'd abandoned the llamas.

"Hey, Doc!" Donald's voice rose in greeting, and several female voices echoed his welcome.

Claire turned away from her knitting for a few seconds. Her hands froze when she saw Dutch in line at the café.

Oh, boy.

She forced out a breath and resumed knitting.

What was he doing here? Couldn't she go *anywhere* without running into him?

"Hey." He gave a quick wave toward the group before he placed his order. Claire noted the pile of books and magazines in his hands. Dutch had always been a reader. Some things didn't change.

But *he* has, she reminded herself. He hadn't seen her yet, she was sure. He would have narrowed his eyes at her, scowled or left. Or all three. He had to deal with her when he tended the llamas. He put up with her so Sasha could visit. But he hadn't previously encountered her out here in civilization.

In the real world.

Too bad. It was high time he accepted that she was a participating member of his community—and that she wasn't going anywhere.

CHAPTER NINE

"GRANDÉ DRIP." Dutch enjoyed the bookshop's home roast whenever he came out to Annapolis, which was pretty often. Since starting up his vet practice he'd made a habit of occasionally getting away from Dovetail and finding some solace in the local bookstores.

Several years ago he'd scoured the shelves—and the Internet—for anything on breast cancer and any glimmer of hope to save Natalie. Before that, he and Natalie had come here to get the baby-raising books she wanted.

He smiled to himself. Even though he was a vet and could've helped Natalie give birth if he'd had to, he'd been more nervous than she was. When Sasha was born at Anne Arundel Medical Center, a short drive down the road, it'd been the happiest day of both their lives.

He paid for his books with the coffee, grabbed the steaming cup and turned to walk by the knitters, toward one of the empty tables. They used to come here on Thursdays, he recalled. He never thought about it much as his days in town were rarely planned.

He looked up as he took a sip of the pungent black coffee and fought not to choke.

His gaze took in the occupant of the worn leather

easy chair near the center coffee table. His first instinct was one he'd rather not acknowledge. He was getting used to it whenever he saw Claire.

Arousal. Interest, of the most basic kind.

He dug for a more appropriate reaction.

What the hell was Claire doing here? In Natalie's old seat, no less.

Son of a bitch.

His hand shook and he gripped the paper cup more tightly.

"Good afternoon, everyone." He kept his voice even, didn't look back at Claire. Her eyes remained downcast, focused on whatever she was knitting.

"Hey, Dutch, I'm going to bring Jasper in tomorrow—he's limping again." Patsy all but drooled at Dutch as she knit her flamboyant multicolored scarf. Her needles were the size of wood stakes and her bright green nails clicked against them as she worked.

"No problem. You still have him on glucosamine?"

"Yes, of course. And the new food you suggested has perked him up." Patsy frowned. "I think that eleven years of chasing geese and rabbits and foxes is catching up with him."

"Aww, he's got a few more goose chases in him—so to speak. I'll check him out tomorrow."

Patsy leaned toward Claire. "Dutch doesn't usually see small animals, but he's always taken care of Jasper for me." Patsy's tone was cajoling and Dutch wanted to groan. That woman kept her husband hopping but still had time to flirt with every guy in town.

Maybe she'll make Claire jealous.

The surge of satisfaction at the thought, however fleeting, was enough to prove his insanity.

Dutch needed to get out of here. He couldn't even look at Claire or nod a casual hello.

"Did you see who's joined us, Doc?" Mrs. Ames pointed her tiny lace needles at Claire.

Cornered, Dutch forced himself to stand still and look at Claire. She raised her head and when her eyes met his he didn't explode with anger or feel the usual rush of hostility.

To his total astonishment, he had to stifle a laugh that threatened to burst through his gulp of coffee.

Judging by Claire's pained expression and the way she gripped whatever she was working on, she didn't want to see him any more than he did her. It'd be worthy of a television sitcom if it weren't so painfully tragic, this mutual revulsion between them.

But you don't really revile her, do you?

"Claire." He nodded, not willing to let any of the townsfolk sense his discomfort.

"Dutch." She went right back to her knitting.

He sent the group a last smile. "Good seeing you all. I imagine we'll all run into one another back in town."

"Bye, Dutch." The group all knew him. And they also knew that Claire was sitting in Natalie's place. Dutch hustled out of the store and made a silent vow never to come back here on a Thursday.

CLAIRE DIDN'T MISS how Dutch had looked down and sipped his coffee as Patsy flirted with him. Nor did she miss how attractively his jeans stretched over his hips, how the button-down white shirt he'd tucked into those same jeans fit his broad frame.

But Claire wasn't like Patsy, thank goodness.

Some people never changed. Wasn't Patsy married—for more than a decade now? But as far as Claire was concerned, Patsy was behaving just like the outrageous flirt she'd been in school. She looked as if she was going to sob as Dutch left the bookstore. Claire wasn't sure if she was more disgusted by Patsy's obvious infatuation with Dutch or by her own response to it. She told herself she had no interest in whoever had the hots for Dutch or vice versa.

Did Dutch have a lover?

"Darn it!" Claire muttered as she threw her knitting down on the table.

"You'll have to rip that one back," Donald commented. Claire met his gaze. If he had a double meaning, his passive expression revealed nothing. As for her knitting, the stitches hadn't come out right for the last three rows. Mr. Black meant she'd have to rip out her work back to the last correct row.

She didn't understand how he could look at her work all the way across the table and know what the problem was.

"How'd you do that?"

"Do what?" Now *this* was the Mr. Black Claire remembered.

"Instantly know what I'd done wrong?"

"Hold up your block."

Claire complied and saw what Donald saw. A huge ripple ran through the center of the square, not part of the cable-stitch pattern she'd taught herself. It indicated that she'd either dropped a stitch, gained one or both.

Claire sighed, excruciatingly aware of the fact that Donald had probably witnessed every second of her reaction to Dutch's presence.

"So do I have to rip out the whole thing?" Her vulnerability made her feel fifteen again. As if the entire group could see Dutch's effect on her.

But only Donald seemed to notice.

"It's called 'frogging' now, Claire." Mrs. Ames piped in from the couch.

"You know, because you riiiippp it out, like 'ribbit,' like a frog!" Caroline Beasley, a bubbly redhead, smiled at her. Caroline had been a grade or two behind Claire and now worked as a CPA in Dovetail.

Mr. Black waited for the others to subside, then continued.

"No sense ripping open any more of the stitches than you need to. Take it back to where you miscounted, then start over from there." Claire looked up at Donald again.

By *stitches* he meant *old wounds* or was her preoccupation with Dutch making her crazy?

His gaze was steady and apparently innocent.

But his mouth was ever so slightly curved, the lines around it a fraction deeper. Enough for Claire to realize she needed to make this man her friend. It was never wise to have an enemy who could read you so well.

"Thanks, Donald." She emphasized his given name. He wasn't Mr. Black anymore; Mr. Black would've told her to read another chapter of *A Tale of Two Cities* to understand the significance of Madame Defarge and her maniacal knitting. Donald let her know with a glance that he didn't miss a trick, but wasn't inclined to push her on it, either.

His kindness was evident in the relaxed way he spoke to her. He didn't want her to feel uncomfortable around him.

"This is always scary." Claire ripped back row after row until she couldn't see the ripples anymore, and the stitches left in the row were the same ones she'd started with.

"It's part of the process, Claire. We all rip back, even after years of knitting."

"Donald, if I didn't know better, I'd think you were still trying to teach me theme and motif, only this time on life."

Donald laughed. "Am I that gauche? It's a good thing I retired, then. I'd really confuse today's kids."

Claire smiled at him. "No, you wouldn't. You were always a wonderful teacher. You cared about your subject and the kids. But you did keep a wall up." Indeed, he'd never been the go-to teacher when a student needed affirmation or advice.

"You understand it now, I assume?" He raised his eyebrows at her. She looked at his face; he was still handsome, the once-dark goatee and full head of hair an elegant shade of silver. Claire saw the years in the wrinkles on his forehead. Years of keeping his private life private, years of ignoring the taunts and snide comments issued by adolescent boys learning about their own sexuality.

"I do. And I still think you're wonderful, Donald."

With that, Claire started her first real friendship since returning to Dovetail.

CLAIRE WAS SCRUBBING down her countertop and glanced out the kitchen window toward the barn for at least the sixth time in five minutes. Dutch's truck was there. Some days she went out and talked to him as he tended to the llamas, other days not—she figured he'd tell her if there was anything she needed to be aware of.

Besides, it was easier to her if she didn't have to face him in person.

Alone.

The past few weeks had passed without incident as Stormy healed from the rough birth, the crias grew stronger by the day, and Sasha fell into a routine of spending time with Claire a couple of afternoons each week.

Claire was proud of keeping her promise to herself. She was available to Sasha, but wasn't consumed by Dutch's moods or her own ruminations on their past.

For the most part.

She threw down the sponge and leaned against the counter.

She hated the total awareness her body had of Dutch. From the moment his truck turned into the drive, a full quarter mile up the road, until he was a mile out from her property, her internal radar seemed to vibrate at a frequency just shy of excruciating.

With another man, other circumstances, she'd be able to let herself enjoy the physical chemistry. But not with Dutch, especially since it was so one-sided. Whatever chemistry they'd had as kids only lingered with *her;* she was certain of it. Even if Dutch saw her as more than a client, his loathing for her and his lack of forgiveness remained impenetrable barriers.

Claire wanted to tell Dutch that it was partly Natalie's decision to let the friendship go. Natalie must've known, somewhere deep in her heart, that Claire still cared for Dutch.

The thought startled Claire. Had she painted Natalie as too naive, too "innocent," to be aware of Claire's feelings?

She wished she could talk to Natalie. But if Natalie were still here, Claire would never have sought out her company after moving back. It would've been too awkward.

Everything that involved Dutch was awkward.

She shifted away from the counter and looked out the kitchen window. Dutch's truck was still there.

"This is ridiculous!" she muttered as she thrust her feet into her waterproof fleece-lined boots. If Dutch was going to come out here, she had to talk to him— and he'd have to face her. She had to let go of the past and be the woman she was today.

He was headed for his truck when her feet hit the gravel pathway.

She stared at him hungrily before he noticed her. Tall, commanding in his work clothes. Not many men looked as good in loose jeans and a sweatshirt, but Dutch pulled it off. The regrets of their history tugged at her.

He stopped for a beat, then went to his truck and got in the front seat. He left the driver's door open, though, and sat half in, half out of the cab. A small concession to her presence.

"Charming," she murmured.

"What's that?" He was working on his laptop, which rested on his thighs.

"Nothing. I wondered how things are going."

He spared her the briefest of glances. His demeanor appeared cool, but his eyes gave him away.

So she *did* affect him. The moment in the cottage hadn't been an aberration.

"I can't thank you enough for everything you've done. You've made this much less of an ordeal than it could've been."

Dutch didn't look up as he typed on his laptop. He half sat on the front seat of his pickup. One long leg hung down to the running board.

"It's my job, Claire."

"I know what your *job* is, Dutch. Can you let down the 'I hate you' wall for a minute?" Her exasperation came out with more force than she'd intended. Dutch raised his eyes and looked at her.

"Okay." Was that amusement in his expression? Contempt?

"I know you have a hard time with me, Dutch, but Sasha—"

"Sasha's my daughter, Claire." His voice was flat, and the emotional drawbridge came back up. His eyes homed in on her, as if she were prey. Or rather, as if her motives with Sasha were his target.

"I'm not trying to get between you and Sasha, or Sasha and Natalie's memory—" at his indrawn hiss, Claire held up her hand "—but it's pretty clear to me that Sasha's benefitting from her time out here. I'm giving her a sense of connection to Natalie at her age. I was the closest to Natalie until…until—"

She didn't finish. They both knew that until Dutch and Natalie made love, Claire had been Natalie's best friend.

Dutch's lips thinned and his chin jutted out.

"Sasha's had enough hurt, enough loss. It's very nice that you want to come in and play the great friend of her mother, but let's face it, Claire, you hadn't been a friend to Natalie for a long time before she died."

She ignored the sting of his accusation. "Maybe not. But I'm here now and I'm filling in the blanks for Sasha—and I can do that better than anyone else. And you *know* it, Dutch. Look how happy she is when she's out here."

Dutch sat still, his right hand on the steering wheel and his left cradling the laptop. He gazed at some unseen object through his windshield.

Tears of frustration burned Claire's eyes.

"Can't you look past your disgust with me and see that this is good for Sasha? She thrives when she comes out here."

Dutch sighed and lowered his head. "I'm aware of that. I also know she's been pulling away from me, bit by bit, this school year. I understand that's all part of her growing up, but… I'm grateful she at least has you to talk to."

His mournful tone sent a shock of compassion

through Claire. She lifted her hand to reach out to him, then let her arm drop back to her side.

"It can't be easy, Dutch, being a single father. You've raised her right—look at how well she's doing in school, how polite she is with other adults. But it's normal for her to pull away now. Isn't it a comfort to you to know she was here instead of running around town with friends and their older siblings? Do you want to see her hanging out at the convenience store, bumming cigarettes or trying to buy beer?"

"No." He closed his laptop and put it on the passenger seat. Then he turned back to Claire. His expression was unreadable, but his eyes blazed with intensity. She gulped in a deep breath. He was angry, but she knew she was close to some kind of compromise. He might crack and admit things were working out.

"So what's the harm in burying the hatchet? I'm not asking for us to be buddies, Dutch, or for you to forgive me. But this—" she waved her hand between them "—has got to give. Sasha doesn't need to feel this constant tension between us. It's not healthy for her."

Dutch's response was nonverbal and lightning-quick. Before Claire could take even a step back from the truck, he jumped down and stood in front of her. The instant proximity startled her, but she felt the heat that emanated from him. Even through his sweatshirt and her jacket, Claire felt his warmth.

She looked up and started to take a step back, but his hands were quicker. He grasped her upper arms and stared into her eyes, making sure he had her full attention.

"You're right, Claire. Sasha needs a woman in her

life—and you're the perfect one, as far as Natalie's history is concerned. But as for you and me, I want to make something clear."

He leaned forward and she saw his eyelashes sweep down against his cheekbones an instant before his lips met hers. Neither domineering nor apologetic, the kiss was certain, brief and hot.

Claire hung on to her control, but only because of the brevity of his kiss. She gave herself a full minute to stand still before she opened her eyes. His gaze remained intense, but now she saw what could have been a reflection of her own face.

Surprise. Bewilderment.

"Why did you do that?"

"Why didn't you fight it?"

They spoke in unison, then reached for each other again.

Unlike the first kiss, this one wasn't so rushed.

Dutch moved his lips over hers as if she were his last grasp on sanity. Claire met his kiss with equal desire. When his hands left her upper arms and buried themselves in her hair, Claire slid her arms up and around his neck. She held on tight.

"You taste so sweet," he told her as he licked first her top, then bottom, lip. He leaned back against the cab of the truck and brought her with him, hip-to-hip.

Claire gasped at the pleasure of the contact. Even in their jeans they fit together perfectly.

Dutch sucked gently on her bottom lip and Claire thought she'd scream in need.

"Dutch." She gasped his name into the spring air, the

last of the day's sun reflecting against the red enamel finish of the truck.

A rumble that carried across the wind and made the ground beneath them tremble broke Claire's reverie.

Claire pulled back and looked at Dutch. "It's a truck driving down the highway—it's not coming up here," she said.

Dutch allowed her one more glimpse of the passion in his eyes before he stretched out his arms and forced Claire to take a step back. He loosened his grip on her arms and lowered his own.

He stayed against the cab. Claire hated the instant cold vulnerability caused by the sudden break of contact between them.

"So much for making things clearer." Dutch sent her a wry grin. "But my point remains, Claire. You don't *disgust* me, not in the least. It would be a lot easier if you did."

He straightened up and put one foot on the running board. She couldn't meet his gaze.

She understood. He felt the attraction, too. But his lack of respect for her, his inability to forgive her—hell, she couldn't let go of their past, either.

Spending time with Sasha, offering Natalie's daughter unconditional love, might give Claire a chance to make peace with her inaction of the past. She had to accept that an easy, friendly relationship with Dutch was never going to be part of the package.

Not as long as his kiss could affect her like *this*.

Dutch rubbed his chin.

"Sasha's at an age where she thinks I need to date.

She's also not blind to the undercurrents between us." Dutch's face had returned to the impassivity she'd grown accustomed to.

"I don't want her getting her hopes up with you, Claire. As much as we share a physical attraction, you and I have too much history. We know each other too well. That means we don't have a future. I won't have Sasha disappointed."

Claire tried to swallow past the lump in her throat. *Do* not *cry in front of him.*

"I realize you probably think your time with Sasha is a way to atone for the time you lost with Natalie. I can't deny you that, especially when it seems to be helping Sasha." He shoved his hands in his jeans pockets. "I need to know you and I can agree on that."

"I get it, Dutch." She ran her hand through her hair in an attempt at a casual gesture. "As they say, 'this too shall pass.' She'll outgrow her infatuation with the idea of a romance between us and accept me as a family friend, period."

She fought the urge to scream at him that she didn't need his permission to make amends to Natalie. And that he didn't have to worry about her assuming there was more to their relationship than there was.

He'd kissed her first, hadn't he?

"Right." He climbed back up into the driver's seat. The physical advantage it gave him was so obvious she had to bite her tongue to keep from making a scathing comment. Wasn't his emotional rejection of her enough?

"Claire, one more thing. Don't overpay her when she

works in the barn. Make her earn her wage—she needs to learn that money doesn't come easily, regardless of the profession."

"Fine." She turned toward the house as soon as she could without appearing rude or as though she was running away from him. But she didn't want to watch him go down the drive like some lovesick teen, either. There was also the matter of the tears scalding her cheeks.

Blinded, she stumbled up to her door. Only when the sound of the engine had faded did she wipe her eyes.

No one ever said atoning for past mistakes was easy.

CHAPTER TEN

DUTCH LOOKED AT THE group of girls sitting around the dining-room table. Didn't they hear how loud they were?

"Sasha. Sasha!" He leaned toward his daughter and when she finally looked up from the MP3 player she was sharing with her friend Lisa, he crooked his finger at her.

"What, Dad?" Man, did he ever recognize her expression. Same one Natalie had worn whenever she was annoyed.

"Aunt Ginny called. She can't make it—her study group has to meet tonight for a big presentation tomorrow."

"That's okay, Dad. I know Aunt Ginny's busy. She can still come for the family party on Sunday, right?"

"Yeah, no problem."

He rubbed the back of his neck. A hot shower would do wonders, but he wouldn't be his own man until tomorrow morning at eleven-thirty when all these princesses left.

"Where's the pizza?" Sasha definitely had the female gene for party throwing.

"I'll go check. It shouldn't be long now." He went over to his laptop and clicked on the icon for the pizza delivery place. That was a frequent occurrence in their home these days. Ever since Natalie had gotten too sick to cook and they were all tired of the few basic meals he'd mastered at that point.

"It's in the box, heading over here." Dutch turned to give Sasha the news, but she was already absorbed in a preteen conversation while simultaneously shoving cheese puffs into her mouth. Her braces—

No.

This was her twelfth birthday party and he wasn't going to be a grouch. She was usually pretty responsible about her food choices—she wanted her braces to produce good results, too. And it was her last Friday night of being eleven. Her birthday was Sunday, but they'd picked Friday night for the sleepover so they wouldn't break up all these families' weekends. Plus, Dutch knew he'd need the remainder of the weekend to recover.

He'd counted on Ginny's being here tonight. Not that he couldn't manage it by himself.

Well, kind of.

The doorbell rang and the girls cheered.

"Pizza delivery boy!"

"Wonder if it's hot?"

"Wonder if *he's* hot!"

Dutch grimaced and chose to believe the girls truly didn't comprehend how adult they sounded. When he'd been in seventh grade all he thought about was baseball and…ah, yes, Claire.

Ever since he'd kissed Claire earlier this week, his

mind had been following a very adult tangent. Dutch was grateful that, as precocious as the girls could be, they couldn't tell what he was thinking.

He reached for his wallet as he opened the door. He'd paid for the pizza online, but still liked to tip in person.

But the tall teenage boy with buzz-cut hair and pierced nose had been replaced by a woman in a lemon-yellow cardigan sweater that covered a tight white T-shirt. His eyes went south to the jeans and leather belt slung low on unmistakably female hips.

"Claire." He was lucky he found her name in the jumble his thoughts had become.

She offered him the quickest of smiles. "Hi. I want to drop this off for Sasha."

She held up a bright pink bag with sparkling silver balloons emblazoned all over it.

"Claire!" Sasha squealed behind him and Dutch moved aside, opening the door wide. "Come on in."

"No, no." Claire raised a hand in protest.

"Yes!" Sasha grabbed Claire's wrist and tugged. "Come meet my friends, Claire."

"Oh! Okay, but only for a minute. I have dinner plans." Her heels clicked on the tile entry as she half jogged past Dutch. He didn't miss the glimpse of pink-polished toes peeking out from her heeled sandals.

Keep a lid on it, man.

Dutch knew his hormones were like red-hot coals, and seeing Claire in dressier clothes—compared to her farm attire—only stoked them.

Of course, Claire in a feed sack would turn him on.

Dutch wanted to stop her from coming too far into their home, but how could he when Sasha had a death grip on Claire's arm? Besides, all of Sasha's friends would think she had a weird dad. Definitely not the impression he wanted to give.

CLAIRE KEPT TELLING herself to breathe. This wasn't about *her,* or her and Dutch. It was about Sasha and her party.

Sasha was turning twelve, a landmark year for a young woman. Claire had figured that by dropping off Sasha's gift tonight, on the way to dinner with her parents, she'd fulfill her need to provide Sasha with some kind of connection to Natalie.

She'd brought Sasha the very thing she'd given Natalie for her twelfth birthday—a cologne set with eau de toilette, talcum powder, bubble bath and lotion. Infused with what was apparently the most popular scent of girls today. Teen Brew wasn't a scent Claire even pretended to like, but from what she'd learned on the Internet and from the drugstore clerk, Teen Brew promised to be one of Sasha's favorite gifts.

"Hey, everyone, this is Claire. She was my mom's best friend when they were our age."

"Cool." A smiling girl with curly brown pigtails smiled at Claire.

"Claire, this is Maddie."

"Nice to meet you, Maddie!" Claire refrained from saying she knew Maddie was Sasha's best friend. She didn't want to embarrass Sasha or hurt any of the other girls' feelings.

"And Naomi." Sasha moved to a girl dressed entirely in black, her hair short and uneven around her pale face. The girl barely looked at Claire, and when she did, Claire was horrified by the amount of eye makeup she wore. Did she *want* to look like Morticia Addams?

"Huh."

"Hi, Naomi." So Dutch had allowed Sasha to invite Naomi, Sasha's childhood friend. Sasha had mentioned to Claire that she and Naomi were developing different interests, taking different paths.

Sasha introduced the rest of the girls, six in total.

Some of them looked up and smiled; others nodded but kept their eyes glued to the movie they were watching on the computer.

Claire turned to Sasha. "I came by to drop off your gift and to wish you a happy birthday. I've got to go—"

"No, wait, Claire, you have to see us do our skit! It's going to be *hilarious*." On cue, five of the girls laughed hysterically. Even Naomi managed a half grin.

Claire kept the smile on her face while her discomfort grew. This was *not* how she'd planned to wish Sasha a happy birthday. She'd intended to drop off the gift, then disappear back into the evening.

Claire silently berated herself for not bringing her gift at a different time. But she'd wanted to have the dinner date with her folks in her hip pocket, to prevent this from turning into anything more than a friendly pit stop.

"Claire has other things to do, Sasha." The vibration of Dutch's baritone piqued Claire's awareness of him. She was standing in the middle of his house, for heaven's sake. Of *course* she was aware of him.

She was aware of Natalie, too. Claire looked around. She believed that even after someone's death, his or her essence stayed behind. Especially someone as deeply loved as Natalie.

Dutch and Sasha wouldn't want her memory to fade, and it showed in all the photos of Natalie that hung on the walls and set on tables.

From the outside, the Craftsman bungalow looked much the same as it had when Dutch and Natalie had bought it after college. But inside...it looked more *Architectural Digest* than Claire would have imagined.

Gleaming wood floors, Shaker furniture, a full-size leather sofa and love seat in the family room. A high ceiling revealed a loft over the living area. Claire wondered if it was an office or another bedroom, then caught herself. She had no business wondering anything about Dutch and Natalie's house.

Dutch and Sasha's house, she mentally corrected.

SASHA LIKED HOW her Dad and Claire looked together. Claire was totally different from the way Sasha remembered Mom, but maybe that was good for Daddy. Anyone too much like Mom would only make him sad. And Sasha was tired of sad.

"I'm really sorry, Dutch. I just stopped by to bring Sasha's gift. I didn't mean to come in and make it such a big deal."

"Didn't you hear the roar from the street?" Phew! Dad had ignored Claire's apology and Sasha was glad. Dad's voice was low, and his comment typical of his jokes, but the tone was the one Sasha was all too familiar with. The "didn't you see it coming, dummy?" attitude that drove her crazy.

Parents were so obtuse. Dad needed to be nicer to Claire. Why didn't he tell her he was glad to have her here?

Claire laughed. Sasha really liked Claire's laugh, and even more, she liked how Dad got that little smile on his face whenever Claire laughed.

"Yes, I heard them from the driveway." Sasha liked how Claire didn't seem to let Daddy's attitude bother her.

Dad looked over and caught Sasha staring at them.

Shoot. Sasha busied herself emptying another bottle of root beer into a plastic cup. If she acted like she didn't care what they were talking about, Daddy would chill.

"How much root beer have you had?" Sasha watched her dad's gaze take in the counter, littered with empty glass bottles. Sasha had insisted on the "good" root beer when they'd gone grocery shopping.

Daddy would've bought that icky stuff in the half-liter plastic containers. Sasha knew she'd never convince Dad to let her have Coke for her party—he was anticaffeine for her until she was an adult. But he'd been a pushover for the expensive root beer.

"This is for Maddie."

"Humph." Daddy didn't seem convinced.

She didn't push her luck. Sasha went back out to the party, leaving Dad and Claire alone. That was the idea, wasn't it?

CLAIRE DIDN'T LIKE the close confines of Dutch's kitchen. She looked around the room, which extended

into a sitting area in front of sliding glass doors. Even
with the breakfast counter, she realized the room wasn't
that small, after all. It was Dutch. He was too big.

She looked back at him.

"I'm not plotting anything here, Dutch. Relax." She
gave a stilted laugh as she tried to heed her own advice.

"I'm not trying to seduce you," she went on. "I want
to be a support to Sasha. I did know Natalie before you
did, and you have to admit I know more about what went
on in her twelve-year-old brain than you possibly
could."

She hadn't meant for that part about trying to seduce
him to slip out, but so be it. He really needed to get a grip.
Was he that wary of her? No doubt he was used to women
finding him attractive—Patsy being a case in point. Since
he'd been the one to establish the boundaries of their relationship, she didn't expect him to be so defensive.

"I don't recall saying I thought you were trying to
seduce me."

"I didn't ask you to kiss me yesterday, either, but you
did." She shrugged her shoulders. "I'm over it. I'm not
taking it for anything it wasn't. Why can't you just
accept that I care about Sasha?"

His eyes glittered. He yanked his eyes away from her
and gazed out the sink window. She followed his line
of sight and instead of inky darkness found herself confronted by a mirror image of the two of them. The reflection jarred her. Dutch, long and lean, his hips against
the counter, was all man. Her profile was completely
feminine, her curves highlighted by her tight sweater
and low-slung jeans.

But their immediate appearance wasn't what put the catch in her throat. It was the palpable energy that ricocheted between them. Neither looked very happy, but they looked *alive*. A contrast she shoved aside for the moment.

"Don't you understand why I'm careful where you're concerned, Claire? Because I *know* you. I know how you behaved not just after Natalie got sick, but years before that. You're a leaver, Claire, and Sasha doesn't need anyone else leaving in her life."

His weary tone didn't match the harsh statement.

"Those are pretty judgmental words at this point, aren't they, Dutch? Does your argument sound as tired to you as it does to me?" She straightened and motioned with her hands.

He stood there, neither moving nor speaking.

"I've been back for two years next week. I'm making a go of the farm and opening my shop by the summer. In the current economy, I'd be crazy to do this if I wasn't sure about it. I'm not going anywhere, no matter how much you wish I would."

At his continued silence, she said, "We were *kids*, Dutch. I know I was stupid to let our relationship go, but I won't apologize for wanting to leave Dovetail and see the world. The fact that we drifted apart and Natalie…" She couldn't finish. "What's done is done."

"Natalie wasn't an afterthought or a coincidence. That's not fair. Tom had died that month and we were two distraught kids."

"I was a kid then, too, Dutch."

"Not when you came back from university a few years later."

"I'd had too much to drink. So had you." But he'd still kept her at arm's length, or tried to.

The heat rose off her chest and up her face as he stared at her. Claire thought she actually saw a glimmer of warmth in his eyes.

Was he finally going to crack?

The ring of the phone broke the tension that sizzled between them.

Dutch reached for the phone and answered, never taking his gaze off Claire. "Dutch Archer."

Claire met his eyes with all the nerve she had. She saw him listening, but his eyes communicated something deeper that she wasn't sure she was ready to face.

Fortunately the call had his attention as he grabbed for a pen and started writing notes.

"Where exactly along the highway? Is it just one? Hmm, I see. I'll be there as quickly as I can."

He hung up and turned to Claire. "Drunk driver piled his pickup into a herd of dairy cows coming in for the night. One animal is dead and two are badly injured— one pregnant."

"How awful! You have to go!"

"Yeah, but I can't leave these girls." He picked up the phone again. "Ginny couldn't make it out to help with the party, but I can call my folks or Mrs. Ames."

"Dutch, stop it." She put her hand on his forearm. "I'll stay here with the girls until you get back. It's not a problem."

He looked at her hand. Before she could pull it back, Dutch covered her hand with his. "What about your dinner date?" he asked.

Claire lifted one shoulder in a shrug. "It's not a date, Dutch. It's with my parents. They'll understand. Besides, they love to go out on their own."

She saw a flicker of something in his eyes—was it gratitude that she was here and available to help?

"It could be several hours. I don't know what I'll find."

"*Hello,* it's me. The one whose llamas you saved. Your professional fee can't come close to making up what I feel I owe you. This is the least I can do."

"Thanks, Claire. I appreciate it. But you don't owe me this."

"Doesn't matter. I *want* to."

Dutch nodded, then went into the other room and told Sasha what had happened. "Claire will stay here with you until I get back," he explained.

Sasha squealed and her girlfriends followed suit. "All right! An all-girls party!"

Dutch barely refrained from shaking his head in bemusement. He looked at her one last time. "I'll call when I know what's going on."

"Don't worry about it. This will be as much fun for me as the girls."

CLAIRE WATCHED DUTCH leave and let out a huge breath when she saw the beams of his headlights sweep across the driveway as he backed out. She surveyed the gaggle of preteens and smiled. "Who wants to do makeovers?"

The next several hours were spent painting toenails, eating pizza—which arrived just after Dutch left— making lots of popcorn and convincing the girls that they could stay up as late as they wanted as long as they put their pajamas on and got into their sleeping bags. Claire agreed to keep the movies going.

After most of the girls had fallen asleep, Sasha stood.

"Can I show you something?" she whispered to Claire.

"Sure."

"It's in Dad's den." Claire rose from the easy chair and followed Sasha into Dutch's office.

"So this is where Rascal's been hiding." She smiled at the dog curled up in his bed. Dutch had brought Rascal out to the farm one day and Claire had immediately loved the dog's soulful expression.

Sasha nodded.

"Yeah, he always comes in here when there's too much going on." Sasha bent over as she spoke and pulled a large wicker basket out from under an end table next to the leather sofa.

Claire squatted beside Sasha on the rug.

"I wanted to ask if you can help me with this."

"What is it?" Claire reached out and fingered the navy cotton yarn. It was hand-knitted.

"A sweater for my dad. Mom never finished it. I want to get it done for him by Father's Day, but I can't work on it here, and I have some questions about how to sew on the arms."

The air whooshed out of Claire's lungs. Whether due to the lateness of the hour or the weight of Sasha's request, tears sprang to her eyes.

"I'm still so new at knitting, Sasha, but I'm sure we can find someone to help us." The image of Mr. Black working on the Scandinavian sweater for his partner appeared in Claire's mind. "As a matter of fact," she said,

"I have the perfect person to ask—he's a master knitter and someone I've known since I went to school here."

"Great! That'd be so cool, Claire. But let's keep it a secret, okay? I really want this to be a surprise. I'll bring the sweater and the rest of the yarn in my back-pack next week."

"Better yet, I'll put it in my car now, and your dad will never be the wiser."

"You're the best, Claire!" Sasha all but knocked Claire over with the ferocity of her hug.

Claire hugged Sasha back. "No, Sasha, *you* are. This is a wonderful idea."

Sasha grinned happily.

"Time to get some sleep, okay? I'll run out right now and put this in my car."

"Okay."

When Claire came back into the house, all the girls were asleep, including Sasha. Claire turned off the TV.

She had no illusions that finishing the sweater Natalie had started for Dutch would give either him or Sasha the closure they needed. But this was important to Sasha, so there was no question she'd do it.

A wave of fatigue swept over her. It had been a long, hard month since the crias were born, and this past week had been the longest. Claire was tired of thinking about her past and anything related to it.

Claire looked at her watch. It was past 3:00 a.m. She'd stretch out on the couch in the den, near the living room where the girls slept, and doze. Dutch probably would be back any moment.

CHAPTER ELEVEN

DUTCH UNLOCKED the side door and tiptoed into the kitchen. The dawn light glowed across the wooden floor. The house was warm and smelled of popcorn, soda pop and pizza. He thought he smelled nail polish remover, too.

Rascal greeted him with a sniff, tail wagging.

"Hey, guy. Sorry I left you alone with all these women. Good boy," he whispered as he rubbed the dog's neck and then straightened. Rascal would be asking to eat in the next hour or so. To ensure some shut-eye without the dog whimpering, Dutch scooped two cups of dog food out of the bin near the door, then refilled Rascal's water dish. Rascal would let himself out via the doggy door he'd installed when Natalie got the sickest—none of them had time to walk the dog.

He walked into the dining room, which was clean except for a couple of plastic cups on the table. Further inspection revealed all six girls practically comatose on the family room floor.

Sasha and the girls slept in sleeping bags. No sign of Claire. His gut tightened. Had she left them alone? No, he'd seen her car when he drove up. He forced out a quiet breath and walked into his study.

Claire lay sprawled on his leather couch. She was on her back, her mouth slightly open. Still in her clothes, she'd only taken off her shoes.

He realized she must be chilled without a blanket. As quietly as possible, he opened the storage ottoman and pulled out a fuzzy polar fleece blanket. She didn't even stir as he covered her with it.

He studied her face. With her hair splayed on the arm of the couch, her expression was completely accessible. The smudges under her eyes told him how late she must've gone to bed, and the tiny crease between her brows indicated stress, even in sleep.

But her beauty was inescapable. The same creamy skin he'd kissed in high school. The same delicious sprinkling of freckles across her nose. Her blond hair was darker and longer than he'd ever seen when she was on television as a reporter.

His fingers itched to touch her face. Her beauty had come into full bloom.

He couldn't believe she'd never married. Well, actually, he could—Claire was a free spirit. But she was one *hot* free spirit. She must've had plenty of opportunities to hook up in D.C., in such a highly visible job.

He breathed in deeply and willed his mind elsewhere. It wouldn't do to allow his emotions related to Claire to surface. He tried to distract his lustful thoughts, reminding himself that she was the one link to Natalie that Sasha craved.

Dutch knew he was in dangerous territory. But it wasn't the threat of a physical enemy that haunted him.

It was the emotions that were evoked by the one woman he'd sworn to write out of his life.

Claire.

Here she was, asleep on his couch, in his den, in the middle of the night. The girls were sound asleep in the television room, guaranteed to stay that way for at least the next few hours.

Temptation ran through him, and it took all his will-power to back up and put mental space between them. For a man who prided himself on his convictions, he sure wasn't doing a great job with this one.

Worse, he was finding it harder and harder to come up with reasons to hold on to those convictions....

Ginny believed that people changed. He hated to admit it, but his little sister might be right....

He settled into the easy chair across from Claire and pulled the ratty throw he kept on it over himself. He sure as hell wasn't going to get any sleep in his bed. The girls might need him, and he didn't want them to wake Claire.

Besides, the view from here was far more interesting.

CLAIRE WOKE to the smell of stale popcorn and dog. As she became more aware she noticed that the blanket that covered her was keeping someone else warm—Rascal. The medium-size dog was snuggled against her.

At some point she'd turned onto her side with her back against the couch frame and Rascal had snuggled up next to her. She didn't remember throwing the blanket on when she'd lain down for what she'd thought would be a brief nap.

She held up her arm and looked at her watch.

Seven in the morning! That must've been some case Dutch had.

She listened—no sound came from the television room. The girls were still out cold, thank goodness.

As Claire rose onto her elbows and sat up, Rascal yawned and tried to snuggle deeper. She laughed and rubbed his head. "You're a sweetie, aren't you?"

The dog didn't look at her, but at the big chair across the room.

Where Dutch slept.

Realization jerked Claire out of her sleepy state. Dutch had come home—when? And how long had he been sleeping in here?

He lay with his feet up in the easy chair, the dim glow of a tiny lamp on the adjacent bookshelf the only light in the room. She'd left it on so she wouldn't trip over anything if the girls called out to her.

Claire studied Dutch's profile. This was the most relaxed she'd seen him since she'd returned to Dovetail. His forehead was marked with lines, and his nose and chin seemed more defined. He looked sexier than hell....

His hair was mussed and she wondered if it was still as coarse as she remembered. She'd only felt the nape of his neck when they'd kissed in her yard that day.

No doubt that was the *last* time she'd ever get to kiss him.

She sighed. They'd never get past their history. But she could go and make some coffee for Dutch. She'd leave it warming for him, along with a note.

Who was she kidding—*she* needed some coffee.

She eased herself around Rascal and slipped between the sofa and the chair to get to the door.

A hand grabbed her wrist.

She looked down into Dutch's blue eyes and saw a sparkle of amusement in their depths.

"You're awake!" she whispered.

"Oh, yeah." He yanked on her arm and she fell into his lap. In an instant she was looking up into his face, very conscious of his morning arousal. "What a nice way to wake up…"

Unlike the kiss by the barn, this was a more welcoming event. Dutch's warm mouth was on a slow, patient journey and his hand caressed her face. Claire felt wanted, desired.

She blamed her lack of resistance on the early hour. Even after almost two years of tending to the llamas at the crack of dawn, Claire didn't consider herself a morning person. It always took her at least two cups of coffee.

"Dutch, the girls," she whispered as he nibbled her chin. "They're going to wake up."

"Then we shouldn't talk or they'll hear us." He kept his focus on her face, her nose, her lips. His lips were firm yet soft, and elicited a curl of longing.

Claire reveled in Dutch's attention, his deft caress. She shifted on his lap and heard the creak of the old leather chair. In Dutch's study. In his house—his and Natalie's home.

Claire pushed against his chest. He didn't fight her, but his puzzled look betrayed his thoughts. He wanted nothing more than to keep making love.

Claire couldn't argue with his desire to be together. But neither could she be with him here, in Natalie's house, with Sasha and her girlfriends sleeping in the next room.

She stood and looked at him. "I believe we had a deal."

"Deal?"

She sighed in exasperation.

"Or maybe we need to make a new one. We're friends, friendly, *not* dating. That's what you asked for." She left him and went to make coffee.

CLAIRE WATCHED Dutch make pancakes and bacon for the girls, who were still asleep in the television room. It was seven-thirty and the girls would leave one by one over the next few hours as their parents came to get them and take them to various sporting and other extra-curricular activities that set the Saturday pace in Dovetail.

Claire sipped her coffee. They'd enjoyed a quiet truce for the past little while. "I need to get going," she said. "I have to take care of the llamas." Still, her body didn't respond as she stayed firmly seated on the breakfast stool.

"I stopped by on my way home. I knew it was late and figured you'd be sleeping. I didn't want you to have to rush back. They're fine, Claire. Finish your coffee."

She stared at him. "Thank you for doing that, Dutch."

"*I* owe *you* thanks for staying with the girls."

"Are you sure you didn't plan it?" She smiled at him. She was determined to return to the safe banter that kept them off difficult subjects.

"No, I didn't plan for one animal to die and two to

need hours of surgery, all because a drunk got in his pickup and went the wrong way."

"Sorry. That's not what I meant." Claire lowered her head and hugged her arms around her chest. She looked up again. "I meant that you didn't have to cope with all the energy that was bouncing off the walls." She sighed. "Will you ever take my comments for what they are?"

"We'll never get past our history, Claire."

"I don't expect to get past it, Dutch. However, I do want to live for today. I can't change my actions, or inactions, of yesterday. I was young—we all were. But obviously it worked out for the best, or you wouldn't have your beautiful daughter."

His eyes glinted as his gaze homed in on her face. Claire hadn't felt such intensity even when she'd faced the angriest of interview subjects.

"If things had gone your way, I would've left Natalie for you." He studied her reaction, and for a split second Claire believed he was right in what he'd said earlier— they'd never be able to let go of their history.

Or rather, *her* history. Her mistakes.

Claire sucked in a breath. The reminder of her appalling behavior that Thanksgiving weekend during her senior year in college cut deep. She swore she could feel blood oozing from what she'd thought was a healed wound.

"That was a stupid night, Dutch. I had too much to drink and acted irresponsibly—to say the least. You were engaged, by the way. You weren't married yet."

"But Natalie was still your best friend."

Claire wanted to put her head in her arms on the

counter, but instead slumped down on the smooth oak stool. She lowered her eyes, but didn't bow her head. She refused to let Dutch see the pain, the humiliation, that remained fresh after a decade and a half.

Yes, she'd tried to seduce him that night. To bring back the magic they'd shared in high school—until he'd made love to Natalie. They'd just found out about the horrific car accident that had claimed Tom.

Claire had adored Natalie's older brother, but Tom had been Dutch's best friend. In a moment of weakness, succumbing to grief and loss, Natalie and Dutch had made love.

Claire had been out of town on one of her many academic field trips. She'd taken her most important relationships—with Dutch and Natalie—for granted and left them when they needed her support the most.

Claire had run from the pain. In her selfish teenage angst, she hadn't put their grief ahead of her own.

Natalie had been the one to console Dutch. And he'd consoled her....

Years later, on a trip home for their wedding, Claire had drunk a few too many cosmopolitans and taken advantage of finding Dutch alone after his bachelor party.

"I know Natalie was a good friend to me, or at least trying to be. I wasn't much of a friend to her at all. I'm quite aware of that."

She looked out the kitchen window, as if some answer would appear and make it all better. "I was stupid, Dutch. You were right to set me straight."

"Setting her straight" had meant telling her that she was behaving like a slut, not the girl he'd known in high school. She'd never forgotten the accusation in Dutch's eyes that night. After a searing kiss, when she'd thought they'd never come up for air, Dutch had pushed her away. He'd told her that he'd made his choice years earlier, not only when he'd cheated on her with Natalie, but after Claire had left Dovetail and never looked back.

"You were on a different path than we were, Claire," he said in a low voice. It wasn't a judgment, but a truthful observation.

"I wanted to see the world." She managed a weak chuckle. "To *conquer* the world."

"Did you?"

"No, but close enough. I learned what I needed to." She gazed into his eyes. "I've found out what really makes me happy. The farm, the llamas, creating my own schedule. Those are just a few of the things I love about being home."

Dutch turned off the burner beneath the frying pan and transferred some bacon to a paper towel. Was he listening to her?

She drummed her fingers on the counter. "I wish I'd had the maturity to be there for Natalie, but I didn't. I wasn't. The fact is, I'm here for Sasha today. It really has nothing to do with you or me, Dutch, other than that you're Sasha's father."

Would he ask why she'd avoided him *and* Natalie after her misguided seduction attempt?

The truth was, it had hurt too much to see Dutch. She'd never gotten over the look of disgust in his eyes that night. She'd lost any hope of ever reviving their childhood bond.

CHAPTER TWELVE

SASHA WOKE UP to the smell of her favorite breakfast. Peanut-butter pancakes and bacon.

She crawled out of her sleeping bag, careful not to step on any of her friends. They were still asleep. She'd dozed off to the sound of Naomi and Maddie talking about why certain boys were cute and others weren't. Naomi had seemed happier than she'd been in a while; Sasha supposed that all the fun things Claire had done with them had cheered Naomi up.

Claire!

Sasha heard her voice. She'd spent the night, after all.

Sasha tiptoed through the dining room and listened at the entrance to the kitchen. She liked hearing Dad's and Claire's voices together.

She liked the idea of her dad and Claire being together, too, but it was going to be hard to convince them.

Dad didn't see Claire the way Sasha did. But Sasha had noticed how he looked at Claire when he didn't think anyone was watching. He said he didn't like her "that way" but he couldn't take his eyes off her.

Claire wasn't as easy to figure out. She never said

anything negative about Dad in front of Sasha, no matter how mad he made her. She didn't really talk about him at all. She kept their conversations on Sasha's school, the llamas or Mom's growing-up years.

Dad's laughter caught Sasha's attention. Her stomach rumbled and she went into the kitchen before she could get caught eavesdropping again.

"Good morning, sunshine!" Dad was dishing up a small stack of pancakes from the griddle. A mound of bacon lay on a plate nearby.

"Mmm, yeah. But mostly tired." She yawned.

Claire smiled at her. "You were up until after two."

"What time is it now?" Claire looked at her watch.

"Eight-thirty—oh my gosh! I've got to get home." Claire looked so pretty with her hair down, even though her clothes were messed up. She must've slept in them.

But Sasha didn't want her to leave. "Don't go yet, Claire. Did you eat breakfast already?"

"Yes, your dad fed me pancakes and bacon, and I've had two cups of coffee." Claire patted her stomach. "I'm stuffed."

"Who made the coffee?" Sasha couldn't help teasing her dad.

Dad smiled. "Claire did."

Sasha laughed. "Figures. Aunt Ginny said she could teach Dad to cook and even bake cupcakes, but coffee's not his thing."

"Hey, give your old man a break. I can make a decent pot of coffee."

"If you use the automatic one with the timer, yeah." Sasha smirked at Dad.

"What's it to you? You don't drink coffee, shrimp."
Dad came over and hugged her tight. Sasha wouldn't let
him do this in front of anyone but Claire or Aunt Ginny.
He seemed to be in an especially good mood this morning.

Sasha turned to Claire. "Dad always buys his coffee in the morning now. Either at the diner or the
doughnut place."

"I see." Claire winked at Sasha, and Sasha liked the
way Claire treated her—as if they were the only two
women who understood the weird side of Dad.

Dad didn't look as tired as he usually did after an all-
nighter. "How'd your case go, Dad?"

He sighed as he poured more batter on the griddle.
"It was long, but I managed to sew up two cows and
save a calf. He just had a scrape compared to his
mother."

"Oooh!" Sasha hated the thought of any animal in
pain, especially a baby. "Will they be okay?"

"I think so."

"Your dad's a master vet, Sasha. If it weren't for
him, my llamas wouldn't have made it." Claire stood
from her stool like she was preparing to leave, but Sasha
didn't want to let her go, not yet.

"You'd already tended to the first twin just fine."
Dad addressed Claire as he flipped the pancakes. Sasha
recognized the tone. It was the "good girl, job well-
done" tone he used when he was really pleased with her.
Sasha wondered if Claire knew what a compliment it
was to have Dad talk to her like that.

"Hey, Dad, is it okay if I show Claire my room?"

Dad's eyebrows rose, but he stayed calm enough. "You didn't show her last night?"

Sasha shrugged. "No, we were too busy down here."

"That's true," Claire said. "But I'll see your room another time, Sasha. I really need to get going."

"It won't be more than a minute." Sasha looked at Dutch. "Please, Dad."

"No problem for me."

Claire still wasn't convinced. "Dutch, if you're sure you're okay with…?"

"Of course. Just don't look at the mess."

"Can't be messier than mine or Natalie's ever were." She laughed, moved toward the stairs and followed Sasha.

Sasha led Claire into her room and twirled around. "It's not too fancy, but I wanted you to see what I did with the pictures I took at the farm." Sasha pointed to the bulletin board over her bed and Claire walked over.

"Oh, Sasha, these are beautiful!" She knelt on the rainbow-patterned comforter and leaned toward the wall. "You've captured the crias so well. Nip and Tuck have grown so much since then! And it was only a month ago." Claire stared at the photos. Then she came to the one Sasha never took down.

Sasha and Mom.

Claire's face grew still and Sasha wished she'd protected her. The picture of Mom with no hair and so pale would be a shock to someone who didn't remember her that way. Sasha hadn't meant to upset Claire or hurt her feelings.

"I'm sorry, Claire. Please don't feel sad. Mom was sick then, but she's in a good place now."

"I know she is, sweetheart. And she loves you very much."

Claire didn't look at Sasha, but kept staring at the photo of her and Mom. Maybe Claire hadn't seen Mom bald. "Had she lost her hair the time you saw her when she was sick?" Sasha asked.

Claire shook her head and got off the bed. "No—I mean, yes, she'd lost it, but it grew back after that. For a while." Claire's face was serious and Sasha wondered if maybe she was tired from last night, too.

"Thanks for showing me your room, Sasha. It's such a lovely place for you to come home to."

"Yeah. I like it."

"And thanks for letting me be at your party." Claire held open her arms and Sasha went to her. They hugged, and Sasha loved that Claire rubbed her back. It felt so nice.

"But you didn't have to stay, you know."

Claire tugged on Sasha's ponytail and pulled away. "It was my privilege, kiddo. I'm going now, but I'll see you soon, out at the farm, okay?"

"Yup!"

"Don't forget we'll be working on the sweater," Claire said in a stage whisper.

"Thanks," Sasha whispered back.

Sasha walked behind Claire as they left the room and went downstairs. Three of the girls sat at the breakfast counter, stuffing their faces with Dad's pancakes.

"Hey, save some for me, you guys!"

She noticed that Dad saw Claire getting ready to leave and he came to stand beside her. He was going to walk her to the front door. Sasha smiled. Maybe Dad and Claire would figure out for themselves that they made a good pair.

DUTCH LET CLAIRE go even though he wanted to grab her arm, make her stay. Was he that lonely for female companionship? Did he actually want more conversations on the subject that was most painful for both of them?

And yet he didn't have any regrets. Claire was right; he had Sasha. And he'd loved Natalie with all his heart. They'd never had the chemistry he and Claire had experienced, but what they'd felt was deep and true.

Claire had been gone the minute she'd found out what happened between him and Natalie. No understanding, no compassion. He couldn't blame her, not when they were kids. But after a few years of college, he thought she'd get over it.

She hadn't. Or at least it seemed that way.

"Claire, are you sure you have to go?" Sasha implored.

"I'm afraid so. You girls have more energy than I do! But I'll see you next week, Sasha." Claire embraced her in a hug, her lips on Sasha's bent head. Like Natalie would have done.

His stomach tensed at the brief wave of pain and awareness. He knew Natalie wasn't coming back. And he knew he was sane—Claire wasn't channeling Natalie's spirit.

But the gesture of female affection from Claire and the way Sasha soaked it up brought tears to his eyes. His sister, Ginny, loved Sasha and Sasha loved her, but it wasn't the same. Ginny was several years younger than him and Claire; she didn't have a parental love for Sasha.

Claire grabbed her sweater from the bench and shrugged it on. She looked back over her shoulder and caught him watching every move. She met his gaze with equanimity, then turned and left.

She closed the door quietly and Dutch sighed. The house seemed colder without her.

THAT AFTERNOON Dutch drove around Dovetail and its environs as he examined his patients with methodical care. Earlier, he and Sasha had cleaned up after the sleepover. Sasha had stayed home, since he didn't plan to be longer than a few hours or so and she was exhausted from the slumber party.

He was grateful for the solo time. He'd been a bit overwhelmed by all the female energy that had invaded his home lately.

He shook his head at the horse he was examining. Sasha's girlfriends weren't the issue. It was Claire.

"How you doing today, old gal?" He stroked the side of the aging mare. He was looking after her for the Browns while they wintered in Florida. They'd be home in a week or so. Usually Dutch left pet sitting to the smaller agencies or one of his assistants. But Goldy had needed antibiotics and he wanted to nurse her back from the infection in her right foreleg.

He led Goldy out to her field to graze, and she placed her nuzzle against him. He laughed, and it felt good to let the joyful sound echo through his chest.

How had he gone from never wanting to see Claire again to allowing his daughter to spend time with her?

To kissing her?

He could forgive himself for the kiss in front of the truck. He'd reacted to her constant presence, the way she got under his skin no matter how carefully he guarded himself. As well, the embrace outside the barn had been pure reaction.

The kiss this morning, though, he had no excuse for. It had simply felt right to pull her onto his lap. She'd welcomed his touch as he'd kissed her. Those kisses had reminded him what making love to a woman who knows you feels like.

Claire knew him—but she didn't know everything.

He'd thought he could never forgive Claire for what she'd done—or not done—with Natalie those last years. He'd made it clear where she stood with him, and Dutch refused to lead a woman on.

Unfortunately, he was having trouble following his own rules.

The Claire he was getting to know bore little resemblance to the Claire of ten and fifteen years ago. He wondered what had brought about the change. It wasn't just about Natalie or Claire's regret over breaking a vow of friendship.

He sighed and watched Goldy clomp around the small patch of fenced-off field. Perhaps Claire had simply grown up. She'd told him that she had finally figured out what made her happy. But it was too late for Claire and Natalie.

And it had to be too late for Claire and him. Didn't it?

"SASHA! DINNER," Dutch shouted. She'd stayed in her room since he'd come back from tending to Goldy.

Dutch handed her the plate he'd filled with meat loaf and broccoli. He was grateful for this dinner together, when she didn't have the pull of a social activity on a Saturday evening.

"No potatoes?" Sasha looked at the plate and her voice rose.

"You just reminded me." Dutch made a quarter turn and opened the microwave door. "Here you go!"

"Thanks, Dad."

They took their usual spots at the counter on their stools. Dutch knew he should use the dining room more often, but this suited them fine.

He mused at how effectively they'd become a team. He would've forgotten the potatoes he'd reheated until he went to use the microwave to make popcorn later, or worse, heat up their oatmeal in the morning.

But Sasha knew that meat loaf wasn't a meal without potatoes.

"So how did you like your party?"

"It was awesome, Dad. The absolute best." Sasha swallowed a huge forkful of potatoes.

"And you felt completely safe with Claire here?" He had to ask it, to assuage any parental guilt.

"Of course!" Her eyebrows tilted up and Dutch saw the wariness in her eyes. Nothing got by Sasha these days. She munched on a roll she'd smeared with butter. "I mean, Dad, Claire would *wallop* anyone who tried to hurt us."

Dutch felt as though someone had punched him in

the gut. Sasha completely trusted Claire. She wasn't always so open with adults outside the family, but she'd included Claire as *part* of their family.

For Sasha to say that Claire would stick up for her as fiercely as he would—that got his attention.

"Why did you ask me that, Dad?"

"I'm a worrier, honey. I always need to be sure that you're safe and comfortable with whoever you're with."

"But you know Claire. You like her, too, don't you, Dad?"

Uh-oh. He heard it. A slightly different tone, but he'd heard it—the implication that he and Claire might have some kind of future.

"Of course I like and trust Claire, Sasha, or I wouldn't let you spend time with her. But you do understand we'll never be more than friends?"

"Sure, Dad." She kept eating and her eyes were downcast, focused on her plate.

Dutch rested his fork on his own plate and leaned closer to Sasha. "I want you to know I'll never try to replace your mom, Sasha." His voice was huskier than he would've liked, his emotions too close to the surface.

Sasha turned to face him and he saw her roll her eyes. So twelve!

"Dad, I *know* that. But it's been…awhile." She looked uncomfortable again.

"It's been awhile since what, Sash?"

Sasha's gaze was clear, honest. "Since Mom left." Her eyes filled with tears, but she carried on. "I know you loved Mom, and she wouldn't have left if she didn't have to. But it's not normal for you to live by yourself for the rest of your life."

Speechless, Dutch stared down at his plate. What Sasha was really saying was that she needed more than the two of them. He knew it was true, but that didn't ease the ache in his chest.

Slim arms reached around his shoulders.

"I love you, Dad, and Mom did, too. But we both want you to be happy."

Dutch turned and hugged Sasha hard.

"Baby girl, you're all I need to be happy. To be sure you're healthy and safe, that's all I need."

"I know, Daddy." Her voice was soothing.

Yes, his little girl knew, all right. She knew too much.

CHAPTER THIRTEEN

SUNDAY MORNING Claire watched the white puffs of cloud race over the barn and fields. She savored the coffee she'd brought outside after she'd tended the llamas.

The sound of crunching gravel drew her attention. No one visited her this early on a Sunday. Maybe it was one of the twins. She immediately discounted that idea as the girls usually slept in after a Saturday night out.

Curiosity took her toward the end of the barn so she'd see her visitors before they saw her.

Dutch's red pickup drove into the yard, and he wasn't alone. Sasha was in the passenger seat.

Claire looked at her watch. It was only ten on Sunday morning.

She walked over to the truck, which was parked near the house. Sasha had already bounded up the farmhouse steps and begun to pound on the side door.

"I'm over here!" Claire shouted. Dutch's head turned and he lowered the passenger window. Sasha came back down the steps, then ran over to Claire.

Sasha's hug made Claire take a step back so they both didn't end up on the grass. Claire laughed and held her coffee mug up so as to not spill on either of them.

"Careful, Sasha, you almost got yourself burned!" She hugged Sasha with one arm, then looked at Dutch. "Is everything okay?" she asked.

Sasha's smile was big and wide. The sun glinted off her braces with their pink wires. Claire was impressed, not for the first time, with how wonderful it would've been to pick the color of her braces when she was Sasha's age.

"Everything's great!"

"That's right—today's the *real* day! Happy birthday. Here—" Claire put her mug on the grass "—let me give you a proper birthday hug."

Sasha hugged her back quickly, then wriggled out of the embrace, unable to contain her news. "We've come to kidnap you!"

"Kidnap me?" Claire frowned at Dutch, who gave her a shrug. His expression said "don't blame me."

"Yes! I get to pick what I want to do on my birthday, and I want you to come to Annapolis with us. Can you?"

Claire stared at Sasha. "Well…I was going to get some of my consulting work done today—" At the crestfallen look on Sasha's face, Claire stopped. "Of course I can come. Let me get a sweater." She hurried over to the truck.

"Whose idea was this?" she asked in a low voice.

"Whose do you think?" The lines around his eyes crinkled and he allowed a full smile to lighten his face. Claire's body reacted in a way that was not "just friends." She loved his obvious delight in pleasing Sasha and what it told her about the kind of dad he was. The kind of *man*.

"Sasha's." She glanced at Dutch's attire. "What I'm wearing is okay?"

"Of course. Dinner afterward will be casual, too."

"Dinner?" Sasha had said they were driving into Annapolis. Lunch, okay, but dinner, too?

"Wait a minute. It's Sasha's birthday. So you're all going to your parents' for her birthday dinner, right?" No way was Claire going to his family's house. She knew her limits.

"Sasha wants Japanese food—sushi—so we'll stay in Annapolis for dinner. You're invited, and no arguing. My parents have been asking about you ever since Sasha started visiting the llamas. And Ginny will be there—she's excited about seeing you again."

Claire's stomach flipped. She and Ginny had always been cordial. She'd never had an issue with Dutch's parents, either. How much they knew about her past with Dutch was a mystery. They'd known her as a child, of course, and then when she and Dutch had dated. But their dating time had been so brief. No more than— what?—three years.

The bigger worry was whether they blamed her for not visiting Natalie, not supporting her.

They all knew she was coming to dinner. If they did harbor a grudge, she didn't stand a chance. However this was *Sasha's* day and she'd be there for Sasha.

"Fine. I'll go collect my purse and a few other things and be right back." She needed time to collect her *wits,* she thought wryly. It was never simple with Dutch.

You're doing this for Sasha.

DUTCH WATCHED CLAIRE climb the steps and marveled at how God had created woman. Especially this woman, with curves that had a power over him he didn't care to admit, even to himself.

"Dad? Do you think Claire's okay with this?" Sasha's voice next to him was worried.

He took his gaze off Claire and looked at his beautiful daughter.

"Of course she is, pumpkin. We surprised her, that's all. Claire is the type who needs some time to absorb it." He hadn't phoned her for precisely this reason. She would've instantly said no.

"You sound like you've been thinking a lot about Claire, Dad."

Dutch tried not to react, although Sasha's observation was all too accurate. She'd caught him staring at Claire a couple of times, and now she saw him watching the farmhouse door like some lovesick puppy.

"I've known her our whole lives, honey." He tugged Sasha's hair. "Don't forget, she's the one who named me Dutch."

"Oh, yeah." Sasha acted casual, but Dutch knew better. His little girl was quickly turning into a wise young lady.

"Do not get any ideas in that head of yours, Sasha." He kept his tone soft but insistent.

"I'm not!" Sasha protested, but he saw the smile on her face and the sparkle in her eyes. He liked her strong will and knew it would serve her well over a lifetime. But some days it gave him a few gray hairs.

SALTY AIR WHIPPED at Claire's cheeks as the tour boat churned through the Chesapeake Bay into the Severn

River. The old vessel hauled around the far corner of the United States Naval Academy, offering the passengers a breathtaking view of its sailing center.

Sasha had picked the excursion as the one "big thing" she wanted to do. The rest of the day would be spent walking around downtown Annapolis and the Naval Academy grounds.

The three of them shared a wooden bench under the awning of the boat. Sasha sat on the port side so she had an unobstructed view. Dutch sat next to her, with Claire on his other side. Claire assumed they'd switch positions when the boat turned around to go back toward Annapolis Harbor. She was trying to keep her stomach steady until then.

She'd refrained from telling Dutch or Sasha that she suffered from motion sickness. It wasn't something Dutch would remember from their childhood. If he did, he probably figured she'd outgrown it. For the most part, she had. Long drives and flights didn't bother her anymore.

But water…

Claire had never developed an affinity for the ocean. Her idea of a great time that involved water was walking along the beach or taking a soak in the tub.

Chugging around the point of the U.S. Naval Academy on a diesel boat, whose fumes would make the staunchest sailor gag, was not even on Claire's list of *possible* good times.

"Dad, look at the mids!" Sasha squealed with delight at a group of midshipmen who were walking together along the seawall.

"They're plebes. Freshmen. Upperclassmen don't have to wear their uniforms on Sunday." Dutch spoke to Sasha before he cast Claire a sidelong glance.

"Do you remember Becky Adams?" he asked. His voice was the only thing that could make her feel better.

"Sure do. We actually ran into each other in D.C. at the Pentagon." Claire hoped he didn't notice that she didn't look at him for very long. She had to keep her eyes on the horizon or the coffee she'd had earlier would make a comeback.

"No kidding?" Dutch laughed. "I never pictured her as the navy type while we were in high school. How'd she do?"

Annoyance made Claire forget her nausea.

"What do you mean, 'navy type'?" She'd never known Dutch to be a chauvinist. Now with a daughter, he hadn't changed his mind, had he? Grown protective in some regressive way?

"She seemed so indecisive when we were in school. Her life revolved around parties, boys and clothes. It's hard to imagine her being part of a military unit, having to put others above herself."

"She's done well. She was even promoted a year early, which in the navy is a huge deal, especially for someone still relatively junior." Claire made sure she had his attention and that his gaze was on her before she spoke. "People *do* change, Dutch."

His expression remained neutral, but she saw the gleam in his eyes. "So I've been told." He looked at her in the same way he had right before he'd kissed her beside his truck. At Sasha's voice he averted his gaze.

"Dad! Check out the huge ship out there!" Dutch turned toward Sasha. A wave of nausea hit Claire and she clung to the post of the awning with both hands. She peered at her watch. The boat tour was supposed to be back in port in ten minutes. Claire stared out at the harbor. She silently prayed that she wouldn't make a fool of herself by throwing up during the cruise.

SASHA WISHED she could learn to keep her mouth shut. Dad had looked like he was going to plant a big smacker on Claire, but because she'd screamed at him about the ship he didn't. Of course, he probably wouldn't kiss another woman in front of her, his *innocent* daughter, anyway.

Sasha wished she'd sat on the other side of Claire, so she could've put some space between her and Dad, and so he'd focus on Claire rather than her. She hadn't thought about it ahead of time. Plus Dad was überprotective and never let her leave his side when they were out, especially in a city. He still thought she was five and would run off and disappear.

"Claire, are you having fun?" she screamed over the engine as they sped in toward the harbor.

"Oh, yes!" Claire answered with a thumbs-up, and then looked back at the shore. She must like being out on the water as much as Sasha did. Claire hadn't looked at anything but the view the entire time.

The cruise was ending way too soon. Sasha loved being out on the water. In her dreams she sometimes sailed on a big beautiful boat with Mom. She hated waking up from those dreams.

Dad told her that they'd taken Mom to Hawaii right after her first round with the cancer and chemo, and Sasha and her mom had gone sailing with Dad. Sasha supposed her dream of Mom and sailing came from that. She'd only been four at the time and she didn't remember much about the actual trip. Dad said she'd gotten strep throat and the antibiotics had made her really sleepy.

"Dad, can we go out for ice cream?"

"Sure, but not until after we get some lunch." Dad was big on eating good stuff first, then the junk. He thought she wouldn't be able to eat as much ice cream if they had a "proper meal" at her favorite sandwich place, but he was wrong. Anyway, it was her twelfth birthday, Claire was with them, and Dad and Claire were getting along great.

Dad turned to Claire. Sasha heard him ask what kind of ice cream she wanted.

Sasha leaned forward to hear Claire's answer.

Claire didn't look so good.

"Ice cream?" Sasha could barely hear Claire over the sound of the engine and the wind. Claire screwed up her face and her hair was all wild and crazy. Sasha was going to laugh, but then Claire whirled around and leaned over the boat's railing.

And barfed.

"Ewww," Sasha couldn't help groaning. *Ick*.

Dad had his hand on Claire's back, his other hand on the railing. Sasha saw that he was rubbing Claire's back like he was trying to make her feel better. That had to be a good sign. It had to mean that he liked Claire more than he realized. Sasha smiled.

Dad turned and noticed her grin. He frowned.

Uh-oh. He thought she was laughing at Claire throwing up. Great. Sometimes Dad *so* didn't get it.

Dad stayed with Claire until the boat pulled up to the pier. "Sasha, get our stuff, will you?" He motioned toward the small backpack that he'd used to carry their camera and water bottles.

"Yeah, sure, Dad." They all got onto the pier and started walking back toward the main part of town.

"Claire, are you okay?"

Claire nodded at Sasha. "Yes, but I'm embarrassed about...what happened. I hope I didn't ruin your big cruise." Claire did look a lot better now that they were on solid ground.

"No, of course you didn't." Sasha turned to Dad. "Can we go get lunch?"

"Sure." Dad wasn't smiling, though. But his arm was around Claire, so that was another good sign. Sasha sidled up to Dad and put her own arm around his waist.

"Thanks, Dad. This is the best day ever!"

"You're welcome, pumpkin." He kissed the top of her head and Sasha smiled. Dad couldn't be that mad considering the way he'd hugged her back.

SOMEHOW DUTCH FOUND himself walking up West Street in Annapolis with a girl on each arm. His daughter fit in snugly beside him, happy that they were heading toward Chick and Ruth's, the landmark fast-food restaurant in the historic part of the city.

And Claire. Claire was under his other arm and finally getting back her usual rosy pink color. He laughed and she glanced up at him with a look that labeled him insane, which only made him laugh more.

"Your face was kind of green out there."

"Thanks, Dutch. I appreciate the support." Her tone was light, and the smile in her eyes let him know she was already getting over her stomach troubles.

"You should've told us you get seasick."

"Are you kidding? It was the most fun I've had on a Sunday in forever. I wouldn't have missed it for the world." Her earnest expression shot a bolt of warmth through him.

She wasn't feeding him a line. She meant it.

He hugged her more firmly, aware of Sasha on the other side. *Talk about balancing the women in your life.*

"Claire, I'm so sorry you got sick," Sasha piped up. "When I'm sick, after I'm sick, I mean—" she smiled her goofy twelve-year-old smile "—I always get really hungry. Maybe it'll help if you eat something."

"That would be wonderful."

Dutch glanced down at Claire and met her eyes.

Her gaze was direct and clear. While she didn't return his embrace, she didn't try to get out from under his arm, either.

And then she smiled at Dutch. Real happiness shone in her eyes.

She's sincere.

"Give me a big old sandwich from Chick and Ruth's and I'll be fine." Claire laughed and broke eye contact with him.

CHAPTER FOURTEEN

ONCE THEY'D ALL squeezed into a tiny booth meant for two, Claire rued that she'd said anything about being able to eat a big meal. The menu at Chick and Ruth's usually enticed her, but between the surprise of Dutch and Sasha bringing her out here, the eventful boat ride and the excitement of being so close to Dutch for such a prolonged time, Claire's nerves were frayed.

Overwrought nerves went straight to her stomach. A bad habit she'd picked up while working in the high-paced world of the White House.

"What are you going to have, birthday girl?" Dutch's voice rumbled next to her.

"I want the Abe Lincoln." The sandwiches at the diner were all named after politicians.

"Old Abe, eh? I think I might go for the Ronald Reagan. What do you want, Claire?"

The heat of his body against her right side put her on full alert. She'd slid into the booth, never thinking Dutch would try to share a seat with her. She'd assumed he and Sasha would sit together, or she and Sasha. But Sasha had claimed a bench all for herself and Dutch got in beside Claire.

"Um, I may get something light. I haven't decided yet."

Dutch's expression changed from teasing curiosity to concern. "Are you feeling sick again?"

"No, I'm fine. I want to make sure I save room for all the food we're going to have later. You did say ice cream and sushi, didn't you?" Claire smiled over at Sasha, who responded with a grin.

"Oh, yeah. Definitely."

Dutch's eyes were still on her. She felt the heat of his gaze.

"Dutch, I'm fine. Today isn't about me. Please don't make a fuss."

"Sasha and I did this you to thank you for staying on Friday night. If you're not feeling well, we need to take care of you."

"Claire, do you want some crackers?" Sasha sprang up and went to the waitress station. She obviously felt comfortable in the restaurant.

"Do you two come here often?" Claire wanted the focus off her and her darned stomach.

"Not really, but Sasha's always loved this place. Who wouldn't?" Dutch smiled as Sasha returned with a basket of individually wrapped crackers.

"That's my girl."

Sasha beamed at her dad's praise. "Claire, do you want some ginger ale with these?"

Claire managed a chuckle. "Iced tea will be fine, thanks."

Her hands shook as she tore the plastic off the saltines and put one in her mouth. The salt tasted heavenly on her tongue and she closed her eyes, taking a minute to savor it.

When she opened them, Dutch and Sasha were staring at her.

"What?"

"Nothing. You look like you still don't feel that great." Sasha tossed her head and leaned down to sip her cola. Dutch had allowed the caffeinated drink because it was Sasha's real birthday and it was daytime.

His presence both warmed and infuriated Claire. She was grateful for his kindness when she'd gotten sick, but why couldn't he keep the focus on his daughter and her birthday?

"I'm fine, really." She threw Dutch a look that she hoped conveyed her boredom with the topic.

"Next time you get to pick what we do." His voice was low, meant for her ears only in the noisy diner. Claire felt her color rise and had an immediate vision of straddling Dutch's hips right here in the booth—no doubt exactly what he *wanted* her to think about.

"Dutch, please. Have some respect." She nodded toward Sasha, who was reading her place mat. Or at least appeared to be—no way of knowing what those twelve-year-old ears were tuned in to.

His chuckle was all male and she became abruptly aware of his scent with its tang of salt air and clean soap...and masculinity. She had to admit it was an instant cure for her nausea.

"I owe you a real date, Claire." Dutch's soft proclamation jolted her and he felt it. But he didn't look at her as Sasha started chatting again and his attention was back on his daughter.

Claire used the opportunity for some serious self-talk.

Dutch was reacting to the joy of the day. His daughter was twelve, happy, and he and Claire were getting along well enough. His mild flirting was a natural part of who he was—when he wasn't so guarded around her.

Take it for what it is, Claire.

THEY SPENT THE HOURS after lunch walking the academy grounds. Sasha especially enjoyed the tomb of John Paul Jones and the fountain between Michelson and Chauvenet halls, which housed the physics, chemistry and mathematics departments. Dutch enjoyed watching his daughter have such a great time. And he enjoyed being near Claire.

He kept catching himself staring at Claire or laughing as he hadn't in years whenever Sasha and Claire shared a joke or ganged up on him. Still, he knew he should tread much more slowly.

Based on the past, Claire was not a woman he should ever trust. But he was tired of holding on to his resentments. They'd fueled an anger that had probably helped him get through the pain of Natalie's sickness and death.

The results, however, were the same. He didn't have anyone to blame for Natalie's illness, and it had never been in his control. None of it.

Today had given him a chance to learn more about Claire and who'd she'd become since returning to Dovetail. He could dredge up all the reasons he owed Claire absolutely nothing, yet he couldn't shake the growing conviction that indeed he owed her a lot.

He owed her for bringing Sasha back to him. Not that he'd lost his daughter, but she'd started to slip away emotionally in the last year. She'd needed a woman to guide her through the trials and tribulations of puberty. Even Ginny wasn't the perfect mentor because they were closer in age than the usual mother and daughter.

Claire *had* changed. He'd witnessed it firsthand since he'd started taking care of her llamas. Since that first night in her barn she'd shown a side of herself he'd never imagined.

He didn't want to look any deeper than that today. It was Sasha's birthday and he'd save his own self-examination for another time.

"Dad?"

"Hmm, baby?" He was sitting on the edge of the wall that dropped from the fountain site to the running track that bordered the water.

"Claire looks like she's having fun now, doesn't she?"

He glanced over at the tulip bed where Claire lingered, a few feet off the path that led toward the Naval Academy Chapel.

"Yes, she does. This was a good call, honey." He pushed his sunglasses up. "But it's your day, Sasha. You didn't pick this for Claire, did you?"

"No, Dad!" She punched him in the ribs. Not as gently as she used to, either.

"Ouch! Go easy on your old man."

"When you stop bossing me around, I will."

"Hey, you two, do I need to break this up?" Claire's laughing tone carried across the courtyard and Dutch looked up to see her walking toward them, hips swinging in her snug-fitting jeans.

"Come on, Sasha, let's head out. It'll be time for

sushi with Grandma and Grandpa before you know it."
Dutch lightly jabbed Sasha's upper arm and stood.

"Can we go through the shops downtown for a bit?"
Sasha never tired of shopping, whether she was actually
buying anything or just looking.

Dutch groaned.

"Dad! It's my day."

Claire smiled at him. He felt as though he didn't
have a care in the world whenever she looked at him like
that. He could get used to it.

"She's got you, Dutch," Claire murmured.

"Yes, she has. Okay, squirt. We'll go *window*-
shopping."

As they made their way toward the academy gate that
led back into town, Dutch took Claire's hand. She
glanced at their joined hands, then at him.

"Just for today, Claire. Let it all go and relax." He
swung on her arm lightly, and he felt her resistance
melt.

"Okay, Dutch. Just for today."

"C'mon, Sasha." He held out his other arm toward
his daughter.

CLAIRE WATCHED the family scene in the Japanese restaurant and sipped her glass of chardonnay. The women
had all ordered wine. Claire noted with respect that
neither Dutch nor his dad chose to drink, as they were
both driving. Ginny had come in with her parents and
planned to spend the evening at their home before going
back to Baltimore in the morning.

Dutch's parents—Dan, Sr., and Joan Archer—hadn't

aged much at all. Their skin was rougher and more lined, from years spent on their boat and in the Maryland sunshine, hiking and working in their beloved garden. They were welcoming to Claire and she appreciated it.

Ginny had laughed and given her a hug as soon as she saw her. Claire was taken aback but quickly realized that Dutch's family didn't harbor any ill feelings toward her.

She surmised that he'd never told them the circumstances of their estrangement in senior year, or more importantly, in the years Natalie was sick. And why should he have? He'd moved on by then.

Keep the past in the past.

"How's the wine?" Dutch leaned across the table.

"Lovely. Crisp and fruity."

"Good. Their sushi is always great but sometimes the wine selection can be tricky."

"Sounds like you've been here quite a bit."

His eyes clouded. "A bit."

So had he brought a date, or dates, here? Or had this been his and Natalie's special place?

"Downtown Annapolis has changed a lot since you lived here, hasn't it, Claire?" Joan smiled at Claire, and she smiled back at the woman who had the same blue eyes as Dutch.

"Yes, it has. I don't remember this restaurant or the coffee shop down the road."

"Well, this place opened fairly recently. Do you remember when, Joan?" Mr. Archer looked at his wife. "Two, three years ago?"

"More like three, I think." Mrs. Archer sipped her wine.

So it hadn't been Natalie and Dutch's place. *Must be where he brings dates.* Claire hated herself for allowing her thoughts to go in that particular direction. It was none of her business what Dutch did with his social life.

"So, Claire dear, tell me how your parents are." Joan wasn't going to let her off the hook completely.

Claire smiled. "They're doing well, thanks for asking. They spend a lot of time away, but with cruising and going on nature vacations. You probably know Mom had a heart scare a couple of years ago, but that's all it was. She's healthier than ever."

"And your dad? I remember he had a bad go of it right after you left for college, didn't he?"

Claire winced inside. He'd had heart problems then, but her parents hadn't told her everything. They'd wanted to protect her after the fiasco of her senior year and the breakup with Dutch.

"He's fine, too. Yes, he had heart surgery back then, but has been fastidious about his nutrition and exercise ever since." Claire laughed. "He's healthier than most men half his age."

"That's wonderful." The next minute Mrs. Archer was distracted by Sasha, thank goodness. "Sasha sweetheart, what kind of sushi did you order?"

DUTCH FLINCHED when his mother brought up that difficult time when he, Natalie and Claire all went off to college. Natalie had turned out not to be pregnant, but they hadn't been quick to tell Claire. Their bond had already wound tight around both their hearts.

And he'd believed his bond with Claire to be irrevocably broken.

Dutch looked at the scene around him. His family acted as if Claire had always been there. No sign of any past disturbance.

Claire's gaze caught his attention. She was seated across from him and the candlelight added to the glow in her eyes.

He could hardly breathe.

God, she was stunning.

"Are you bored?" He kept his voice subdued. Since they were at the end of the table and Ginny was engaged with Sasha and his parents, they had relative privacy.

"Not at all. I love being on the hot seat with your family." She smiled as she spoke, though, and surprised him when she grabbed his hand.

"This is a special evening for your family and Sasha, and I'm honored to be part of it." She knew him well enough to understand that he didn't want her to feel like an outsider, or worse, an outcast.

Not many people in his life had ever read him so easily.

He didn't reply. He couldn't. A thought that he'd kept buried for many years whispered in his mind. But it wasn't a soft lover's whisper. It was the voice of his conscience.

Maybe you're the one who doesn't deserve to be forgiven. Not Claire.

He dragged his eyes from her and looked down the table at Sasha, who was animated as she told her grandparents and aunt about Claire's getting sick on the boat.

Dutch groaned. "I'm sorry, Claire. Everyone didn't need to know about that."

"It's okay, really." She waved her hand. "Relax."

Relaxing around Claire when he was so aware of her

was difficult. He'd had to fight off his arousal all day. His daydreams were of being alone with her—soon.

"Tell you what," he said. "I'll make this up to you. I'll take you out, only the two of us, and we'll have a wonderful meal at, let's see..." He pulled on his bottom lip as he thought. "Café Normandie or Yellow Fin, perhaps?"

Claire's eyes widened and she raised an eyebrow.

Both restaurants fell into the *"real date"* category. "You owe me nothing, Dutch. Let's enjoy this celebration."

She might as well have thrown her glass of water at him.

It was sobering to have her remind him of the agreement *he'd* insisted on.

Dutch smiled as Sasha opened her gifts, including the charm bracelet he'd bought her. He hugged her when she ran up to him and squealed her thanks. But he couldn't keep his mind from racing.

Until now, he hadn't recognized a crucial element in their relationship. Claire had changed. And Sasha loved Claire.

So where did that leave him and Claire?

CHAPTER FIFTEEN

SASHA WAS STILL tired on Tuesday after her birthday weekend.

She half listened to Naomi as she droned on about her conversation with Nathan in third period. Sasha liked to look out the window as the yellow school bus made its way through Dovetail. Today she was going to Claire's to help with the llamas.

At least, that was what Daddy thought. And truly, she did work with the llamas, but she also spent quite a bit of time with Claire in her house or more recently, in the small cottage where Claire was setting up her yarn shop. They were working on the sweater and Claire said a friend was coming over to help them.

"You really think so?" Naomi prodded Sasha.

"What? Um, yeah." She hoped her encouragement was all Naomi needed. Naomi was a nice girl under all her complaining and whining, but she had a lot of problems. Sasha didn't care that Naomi had cut her hair spike-short and dyed it blacker than coal, a sharp contrast to her pale skin and sky-blue eyes. And she had to admit the pierced eyebrow wasn't something she wanted, but if Naomi liked it, that was all that mattered.

It was Naomi's annoying habit of going on and on with her "poor me" complaints that drove Sasha crazy. Sasha wasn't always happy with herself, but she knew her dad, Grandma and Grandpa Archer and Aunt Ginny loved her. And now she could add Claire to that list. She smiled.

And then looked at Naomi.

No one else would sit with Naomi. Sasha had invited her to the sleepover birthday party because she liked having all her friends around her. But a couple of the other girls had made it clear that Naomi freaked them out.

"I mean, if he thought it was going to impress me that he reads graphic novels, that's pretty lame, isn't it?" Naomi went on.

"Yeah—obviously." Phew. Sasha had picked up the gist of the conversation. Naomi was still talking about her current crush, Nathan. Naomi acted as if she didn't like him, but Sasha knew that if Naomi didn't like someone she didn't bother talking about him or her.

"That's what I figured." As Naomi thrust a hand through her hair, the jacket sleeve fell back and Sasha caught a glimpse of her pale forearm.

"Naomi, what happened?" She gasped out the question. There were angry red scratches on Naomi's translucent skin. Deep scratches.

"Nothing. I mean, it's from the prickly bush in front of our house."

"What did you do, skateboard into it?" Naomi had been the best skateboarder in their neighborhood, but

Sasha hadn't seen her on her board for quite a while. Not since last summer, anyway.

"Yeah, whatever." Naomi turned back into her despondent self. Sasha was bothered by this side of Naomi, but tolerated it because she felt she saw past the facade. Sasha had liked the word *facade* ever since she'd heard it on the trip to downtown Annapolis with Dad and Claire. The historical buildings in Annapolis often had facades.

The bus stopped where Sasha and Naomi normally got off. When Sasha didn't move into the aisle, Naomi looked at her quizzically.

"I get off at Llama Fiber Haven today."

"Oh, right." Naomi walked down the aisle without a goodbye and climbed out of the bus.

Sasha watched her friend walk into their neighborhood, head down. Naomi sure had been acting weird, ever since she'd quit gymnastics last month. She'd really pissed off her parents, who wanted Naomi to be a "major competitor" in gymnastics.

Naomi wanted more time to chill, but Mr. and Mrs. Roberts had flipped out and grounded Naomi for a month.

Sasha's thoughts turned to Claire as the bus left from the town center and headed out to the country highway. There were only a handful of kids still on the bus. Sasha knew several of them, but no one very well—they were from the outskirts of town, whereas Sasha had grown up in one of the established neighborhoods in Dovetail.

Sasha all but leaped off the bus when it ground to a halt in front of the Llama Fiber Haven sign. With a toss of her ponytail she bounced down the gravel road to

Claire's house. Before she went past the front cottage, Claire appeared on the small porch and waved.

"Hey, Sasha! I'm in here—come on in."

"Hey." Sasha climbed the two steps and entered the cottage behind Claire. The place had been musty and dank last week, but now it seemed brighter, cleaner. Claire wore rubber cleaning gloves and there was a big bucket of sudsy water in the middle of the floor. That explained the difference.

"Wow, Claire, this is great! Do you want me to do anything?"

"I'm almost finished with the cleaning. I thought we could start stocking the shelves with some of the yarn that's come in, then we'll sit down and work on your dad's sweater until Mr. Black comes over to help us." Donald was often part of their knitting time, and he and Sasha had a great rapport.

"Okay. Where's the yarn?" Sasha looked around the room. The rows of shelves were all new, sort of like a bookstore.

"See those boxes in the corner? If we take it one by one, we'll get it unpacked in no time. We'll keep the yarn in plastic bags for now, but at least we can inventory what's here." Claire wiped her forehead with the back of her arm.

Sasha liked how Claire's skin was pink and her hair all wavy around her face. Sasha often tried to curl her own hair, but it was stick-straight, like her dad's.

"No problem." Sasha went to the corner and Claire followed her.

"You know I owe this all to you, kiddo."

"What?"

"This store." Claire tucked a strand of Sasha's hair behind her ear. Sasha loved when Claire did stuff like that.

"I wanted to have a yarn shop eventually, but not until I was on my feet with the llamas. Plus, there was the issue of being able to knit myself. You've taught me so much, Sasha!"

Sasha felt her face grow hot, but she wasn't embarrassed. She was proud she'd helped Claire.

"Thanks, Claire."

"Don't thank me, honey. Thank your mother for teaching you how to knit."

"So, it's like she's the one who taught you, isn't it, Claire?" Sasha smiled at her.

Claire's face stilled and she bit her bottom lip. Sasha always did that, too, when she didn't want to cry.

"Are you okay, Claire?"

Claire wrapped her arms around Sasha. "I'm more than okay, Sasha." Sasha slipped her arms around Claire's middle.

"I love you, Claire."

Claire's breath stopped and it sounded as if she hiccupped. "I love you, too, pumpkin."

"Am I interrupting a female moment?" Mr. Black's smooth voice came from the open doorway.

"Not at all." Claire straightened up, walked over to Mr. Black and gave him a peck on the cheek. It was obvious to Sasha that Claire loved being around him. He was so funny whenever they knitted together.

Sasha loved Mr. Black, too. He told the best stories

while they worked and taught her about the history of knitting.

"Hi, Claire, darling." He kissed Claire on both of her cheeks, in that European style. His twinkling eyes focused on Sasha. "And how's our princess?"

Sasha wouldn't normally like it if anyone else called her a princess—she was twelve, after all. But Mr. Black said it in a nice way, not a sarcastic way.

"I'm fine, thanks." She grinned at him. "Do you really think we can finish the sweater by Father's Day?"

"Father's Day? That's in June." Mr. Black nodded. "We'll have this done well before then."

"Don't forget we'll have to take a break when we get closer to the Sheep and Wool Festival," Claire said. Then she motioned to the chairs around the huge oak table she'd bought for the store.

"Let's sit down and get started."

CLAIRE AND SASHA worked with Mr. Black for an hour or so in the cottage. They'd finally gotten past the difficult parts of the sweater. All that remained was to finish one sleeve and then sew the pieces of the sweater together.

"I'm afraid I can't stay any longer today. Jim's getting home from work late and I need to start dinner."

"Donald, thank you so much for the time you've given us. It's made a huge difference."

"Glad to help." He looked at Claire and winked. "I have a feeling the recipient's going to appreciate this more than you can imagine."

Claire sighed. "We'll see." Did he sense the hope that had started to unfurl in her heart?

CLAIRE LOOKED at Sasha with a smile. They'd finished stacking yarn after Donald left. Sasha had organized the various packages of yarn according to fiber content and color. She was a natural with anything fiber-related, that was for sure.

"Want to have some cookies?"

"Yeah!" Sasha didn't hesitate.

They walked up to the house together, the daylight still bright and the birds singing incessantly from the surrounding trees.

"Look!" Claire pointed to a hawk flying low. She didn't regret serving her years on the job, but she wouldn't trade an afternoon like this to go back to D.C. for anything.

"Cool." Sasha's tone indicated that she comprehended the awe of the bird's territorial swoop. She leaned back to watch the raptor, its red tail glistening gold in the sunlight. Her huge backpack was incongruous as it hung on her thin frame. She looked as if she'd tip over backward with the slightest breeze.

"Isn't that backpack awfully heavy?"

"No, I'm used to it." Sasha straightened and started walking with Claire again.

"I don't get it. I don't remember ever carrying around such a huge backpack, even in high school."

"Yeah, Dad and Aunt Ginny always say the same thing." Sasha shrugged. "We don't use our lockers— they're too small. Plus it's easy to forget a book, and then you get in trouble the next day 'cause your homework isn't done. It's easier just to carry everything with you."

"You don't use your lockers?" Getting her own

locker in seventh grade had been a highlight of middle school for Claire.

"No, it takes too long to get to them between classes. We only have three minutes."

Sasha stopped and stared at Claire. "What did you and my mom do?"

Ah, yes, Natalie. Sasha's connection with Natalie. Claire had to keep that firmly in her mind. Or else it would kill her when Sasha decided she'd learned all she could about Natalie. Like it or not, the day would come when Sasha didn't need her anymore. When she didn't need these wonderful afternoons of sharing and working side by side.

Claire ignored the tug of grief and smiled at Sasha. "We had backpacks, but the most we ever carried was one or two books, maybe a folder. Between classes we'd carry a binder with books piled on top of it in our arms. We put gym clothes and bathing suits in the backpacks."

"Bathing suits?"

"Yes, we had swimming in gym class. Don't you?"

"No, but I think they do at the high school."

"Oh." Claire had assumed the new building would've been bigger and better than the old one where she, Dutch and Natalie had attended middle school.

As they resumed walking, the house came into sight. Claire liked how it stood back from the road and the welcoming vision it offered.

A school memory popped up and she laughed.

"I remember one time when we'd all started wearing bras. Your mom and I had bought ours together at the discount store in South River." Claire bent and pulled a blade of grass up and twirled it in her fingers.

"Somehow when we got back home, we mixed the bags up. I couldn't figure out why my bra was so tight, and your mom had to use safety pins to make hers stay on."

Claire had blossomed early and still maintained her more buxom, athletic build. Natalie had been petite and, back in sixth grade, waifish.

"We had to change before and after gym, and one of the other girls saw my back and said 'Claire, your bra's digging into your skin.' I was mortified.

"Another girl noticed your mom, with her bra hanging from her, and the safety pins. Natalie said, 'My Mom got it big enough to grow into.' Girls of that age, as I'm sure you know, can be really cruel, and one smart-mouth made a comment that your mom needed to stuff her bra."

Sasha's eyes were huge as she'd obviously never heard this story.

"Your mother may have been small, but she let that girl know she'd be stuffing her mouth with her fist if she didn't shut up. The girl never bothered her again."

"My mom was that tough?"

"Oh, yeah. If it hadn't been for her, I don't know how I would've made it through middle or high school. Even though she was the half-pint and I was a bit of an Amazon for those years. She was the stronger, more vocal one. She knew how to stick up for herself and her friends."

"Wow." Sasha stared at the ground as she absorbed this facet of her mother.

"I'll bet you're like that," Claire said. "Are there friends you're helping out?"

"Yeah, sure. I mean, we all help one another out. Like when Katie Kirkland got her hair cut and it wasn't that great but we—the girls—all said it was pretty. We all basically told Melanie Danitti to shut up when she was making fun of Katie. Melanie's always bothering somebody."

"I've found over the years that the people who cause the most commotion often need the most love." Claire thought about what she'd said; she didn't want Sasha to get the wrong impression. "I don't mean you should *ever* put up with someone else's abuse, even if it seems like regular teasing. But it helps me to realize that the other person is hurting, so that I can let it go more easily."

"Yeah, I had a girlfriend when school started who was so nice, but she never wanted to do what I wanted to. She'd try to meet at the convenience store, which my dad would, like, never let me do, and all she did was complain about her parents."

"Let me guess—she wanted to meet boys, too?"

"Duh." Sasha's ponytail bounced in response to her nod.

"Are you still friends with her?"

Sash squinted and her lips pulled down.

"No, not really. But it's not like I'm mean to her. If she wants to sit with me at lunch I don't move to another table or anything. But I don't hang out with her after school."

"I'd say that's a good decision on your part."

They'd reached the house and Claire was impressed

with the mature way Sasha handled her relationships.
She was so easygoing about it, too. Claire didn't remember any of middle school as easygoing, except for
the time she and Natalie were together.

THEY SPENT THE NEXT hour drinking milk and eating
cookies, laughing, and then ended up out in the barn
tending to the llamas. Both crias were doing so well,
Claire couldn't get over the difference only a month had
made. She'd come so close to losing all three.

Stormy contentedly chewed her grains, while Nip
and Tuck frolicked a few feet away. Claire fought the
urge to jump in and help Sasha with cleaning the drop-
pings out of the stables. Sasha needed the experience
for her 4-H project. She *didn't* need an adult hovering
over her every move.

"While you finish up out here, I'm going to run up
to the house to check my e-mail." She was awaiting a
new consulting contract. "You're okay out here for a
couple of minutes, right?"

"Yeah, of course." Sasha kept raking.

Claire headed for the house. The impending sunset
spread out around her as golden rays broke through the
oak trees that lined the short drive between the barn
and the house.

She had a sense of serenity she hadn't felt in a long
time, if ever. She was living her dream and making up
for the sins of the past. While she'd never completely
compensate for abandoning her friendship with Natalie
during those last critical years, this time with Natalie's
daughter made a difference.

Claire wasn't in the house more than a few minutes, enough time to check her e-mail and see that she didn't have the new contract yet. She grabbed a sweatshirt and went back out to the barn.

The gleam of the remaining daylight reflected off Dutch's red pickup, startling her. He was parked next to the barn. She looked at her watch. He wasn't due for another twenty minutes or so.

When Claire walked into the barn she didn't know if the wave of apprehension she felt came from Dutch arriving early or the tone of his voice as he addressed Sasha.

"You've been out here by yourself for *how* long?"

"Only a few minutes, Dad. Claire went back to the house to check her e-mail. She'll be right back. We've been out here together for the past hour."

"I don't care if it's a few minutes or an hour, Sasha. You're supposed to have your cell phone with you at all times."

"Dad!" Her voice had the adolescent tone she rarely used with Claire. The "you're driving me crazy with your ignorance" tone.

"I left it in my backpack, up at the house. I've been with Claire the whole time, Dad. You knew I was here, so what's the big deal?"

"The *big deal*, young lady, is that I've been trying to call you for over an hour. I wanted to make sure you got here safely, and I needed to tell you I might be late. As it turns out I got done faster than I expected, so I decided to come and get you early."

"*Dad!* I'm supposed to have two hours of service with

the llamas each week. I still have another fifteen minutes."

"Working on your 4-H project is a privilege, Sasha. If you can't obey simple rules about using your cell phone to stay in touch, instead of texting all your buddies, 4-H and every other extra activity is going bye-bye."

"Dad!"

CHAPTER SIXTEEN

CLAIRE CLEARED her throat and walked into view of both father and daughter.

Dutch's gaze immediately locked on hers. "Why did you leave her alone?" he demanded just as she said, "Hi."

No way was she going to let him rattle her. She'd done nothing wrong. Neither had Sasha.

They'd spoken at once, and Claire's attempt at a neutral greeting was swallowed whole by Dutch's accusation.

"She wasn't really alone, Dutch. I was gone for only a few minutes."

"What would've happened if she needed you? Could you hear her from here?" Dutch turned to Sasha. "Could you have called Claire on your cell? No."

He turned back to Claire.

"We have strict rules about Sasha's cell phone, no matter where she is. I need to be able to get hold of her, and vice versa, at any time."

"Sure, that's a good idea." Claire looked at Sasha and immediately felt torn. She wanted to be Sasha's ally, but Dutch's concern was legitimate. Although she did think he was overreacting....

"I'll make sure Sasha carries her cell phone when she's here."

"Sasha's a big girl. Right, Sash? You can remember to carry your cell." Dutch's tone was softening slightly.

"Yes, Dad." Sasha's face reflected the glumness of her reply.

"You're almost done here, Sasha. Why don't you finish up and meet me and your dad out in the drive in a few minutes?" Claire told herself it wasn't her place to chew Dutch out for being so harsh with Sasha. He was the father, and she understood that he had to put his daughter's safety first.

It felt as if he didn't trust her, though. That stung.

She grabbed Dutch's elbow and nudged him toward the barn door. He stiffened, but didn't fight her touch.

"Can I talk to you for a minute? Alone?" Claire kept her voice steady as she measured the extent of Dutch's anger. She'd done this before—figured out how close to the edge an interview subject was so she could gauge how far she had to go before that person would break and share his or her feelings without reservation.

Dutch wasn't a congressman or the president. Yet he made her aware of her breath, her heartbeat, her need. Dutch made her shake with anxiety, knowing he'd never let their original feelings for each other resurface. He'd lost too much and wouldn't allow himself to be vulnerable, especially to her.

She reminded herself that this was for Natalie but, even more so, for Sasha. Sasha needed time with Claire; it gave her insight into her mother she wouldn't get elsewhere.

Once they were out of Sasha's earshot and line of vision, she spoke. "Dutch, I know you're upset. And you have every right to be."

His eyes narrowed as he tempered his anger.

"I would never have left Sasha out here if I didn't think she was safe," Claire said, stepping closer.

"I'm not used to all the rules kids have nowadays. But let me know and I'll do whatever you want me to, whatever will make you the most comfortable with Sasha spending time here."

"It's not about my comfort, Claire. It's about her safety!" His eyes blazed with fury and pent-up frustration. He shoved his hands in his jeans pockets.

She stared at him, unable to respond.

"You still don't get it, do you, Claire?" His words hung between them.

"I—"

"It's always been about *you,* Claire," he broke in. "What *you* need, what you want to study, what you want for your life. You don't know a thing about kids. You've been single all these years."

At the unfairness of his words, her spine straightened.

"Being single and living alone doesn't mean I'm unaware of what a child needs or how to keep her safe."

His gaze never left her eyes. He'd convicted her without even a trial.

"I'm not talking about now, Claire." His mouth thinned. "You never got it when Tom died. You said you did. And after a while you seemed to get over what had happened between Natalie and me. But you never truly forgave us. You didn't care enough. You never even talked to me after that. You threw both of us away that easily."

"Hardly!" she snapped, coming to her own defense. "*You* were the one who chose to comfort Natalie that night."

"We were kids. We let our emotions and hormones carry us away." He shook his head. "Everything you've ever done has been planned for, executed, each goal achieved. There's no room for human shortcomings in your life, is there?"

Claire stayed silent. Not usual for her, but she knew that everything he said was true—at least until she'd moved back to Dovetail. She'd accused herself of the same things countless times.

Dutch pulled a hand out of his pocket and raked it through his hair. "I understand why you never forgave me, Claire. But Natalie was your best friend. You were her rock during her childhood, when her parents split up, and for a while right after Tom died. But you had to go on that debate trip, didn't you? And then you weren't there anymore."

"Dutch, I *did* forgive both of you a long time ago, although I'm not sure you've forgiven me. But what happened wasn't totally my fault, either." She finally verbalized the conclusion she'd come to over the past couple of months.

"You and I had already drifted apart when you and Natalie got together. Our choices, *each* of our choices, made our destiny for us."

Claire watched Dutch as his wary gaze stilled and comprehension dawned.

"I'm not asking you to forgive me for leaving town and not being here for Natalie at the end, Dutch. As a matter of fact, I'm not asking your forgiveness for anything. If you choose to continue taking offense at my actions or inactions, so be it. As for me, I'm grateful for this time with Sasha, but I don't want it to cause friction between you. I'm doing this for myself as much as for her."

At his obstinate stance and hard-boiled expression, her anger simmered and she wasn't sure she could control it anymore.

She noticed a movement in the barn. Sasha was talking to one of the llamas and laughing.

Sasha.

Claire turned her gaze back on Dutch.

"You're right, Dutch. I've been a selfish bitch at times. But not all of what I've done is bad. If the worst thing I did was let go of my childhood friends…did it ever occur to you that maybe it's what I needed to do to find myself? As much as you and Natalie needed to stay in Dovetail, near each other?"

"Natalie didn't live long enough to find herself, Claire. She wasn't given that choice."

"You're wrong, Dutch. Natalie lived the life she chose. She studied history the way she'd dreamed, had the baby she wanted, had you." She waited a moment, allowed her words to register for Dutch.

"Natalie's dead, Dutch. Nothing I do, or you do, will bring her back. It's no one's fault that she died, and I'm not taking your misplaced blame and anger anymore."

"This isn't going anywhere." Dutch turned toward the barn.

Claire touched his shoulder and he turned back toward her. "No, wait. I'm not done yet, Dutch."

"No, I imagine you're not." His expression was guarded, but his voice softer. Claire knew this was when she had to press her point.

"I've changed my life, started over. I can be a presence in Sasha's life that will make a difference. A good difference, Dutch. I'm not a monster, for heaven's sake. I'm a woman who's made some mistakes."

The anger roiled slow and hot in her belly. Her hands started to shake. "And you know what, Dutch? I don't need your forgiveness or your approval. For anything." She swept her hands in front of her as if clearing a table.

"All I care about now is doing the right thing by Natalie and doing what I can for Sasha. But if it's going to upset you this much, it isn't worth it. Not for any of us."

She left him standing alone when she strode back to the barn.

A WEEK LATER, Claire made it home with fifteen minutes to spare before Sasha got off the school bus. She gathered up her notes and the supplies they needed for Sasha to practice her 4-H presentation. Since Donald Black wasn't coming out this week, she'd agreed to help Sasha with the llama project. Sasha wanted to surprise Dutch by having the 4-H project done early, well before the Sheep and Wool Festival.

Sasha was going to show Nip at the Maryland Sheep and Wool Festival. Because of the cria twins' rocky start, Sasha had procured special permission to enter the competition with Nip, even though he lived at Claire's barn and wasn't in Sasha's complete control.

Claire met Sasha in front of the barn.

"Hey!" Sasha leaned into Claire in what Claire had come to learn was a sixth-grader's version of a hug. No arms, but Sasha's head rested on Claire's shoulder long enough for Claire to know it was an intentional gesture. Claire gave Sasha a quick squeeze.

"How was your day?" They walked into the barn together and Sasha shrugged out of her backpack.

"Oh, fine." She dropped the heavy bag on the bench outside Nip and Tuck's pen. "Actually, it wasn't that great."

"What happened?" Claire was careful to keep her voice steady, her focus on opening the latch to the cria pen. One thing she'd learned over the past month was that Sasha was more likely to open up if Claire didn't appear too interested.

"Remember I told you about my friend Naomi?"

"The girl who wore the dark makeup?" No doubt without her parents' permission. "I met her at your sleepover, didn't I?"

"Yeah. Well, she's been trying to go out with this creepy eighth-grader. He's a regular sleazebag and he won't have anything to do with her. So now she's going totally bonkers and it's freaking me out."

"What do you mean *bonkers?* Is she overly emotional?"

Sasha looked at Claire as if she were a fossilized dodo bird.

"Kind of, but, you know, more like someone who's a Goth but also sometimes cuts."

"Cuts? You don't mean *cuts class,* do you, Sasha?"

Claire held her breath. She knew what cutting meant but needed to make sure Sasha understood the significance of it.

"No, kids who are lonely or sad sometimes cut themselves to feel physical pain, because it's, like, the only thing that'll break through their, like, emotional numbness."

Her frown and fidgety motion as she worked with the llamas tipped Claire off to how much this bothered Sasha. Her frequent use of *like* also told Claire how agitated she was.

"Where did you learn about this?"

"About Naomi?" Sasha looked up from her chores.

"No, about cutting." Claire stood in front of her.

"Well…" Sasha leaned on her rake. "All the kids talk about it and then in health class Mr. Papadago brought in the school counselor, Ms. Nosette, and she had a talk with us and told us about it."

Claire's insides shook with fear, but she maintained an even tone. She had to or risk missing something important.

"Does your dad know?"

"Well, yeah, I think so. I mean, most people aren't worried about it. But Ms. Nosette said she wanted us to look out for anyone who seemed like they were more upset than normal."

"Did you tell your dad about Naomi? Did you mention it to anyone else, like one of your teachers? This is serious, Sasha. Naomi may need professional help and you may be her only link to it."

"No, it's not like I've actually seen her cut herself. She's acting like she's upset, but I don't think she'll really do anything." Sasha started raking again, then paused. "You know, she had all these scratches on her arms a while back, but she said they were from the bushes near her house."

Claire sighed and stroked Tuck's neck while Sasha tended to Nip. "Sometimes we can't tell what someone will or won't do, Sasha. You could talk to your dad and he could call Naomi's folks."

"Yeah, well, Naomi's parents don't give a crap."

Claire was sure Dutch wouldn't approve of that language, but she needed to reach Sasha. Hoped to, anyhow. She'd fill Dutch in later.

"That's too bad. You know you can always tell your school counselor or nurse, too."

"Yeah, I know. I really don't think she's losing it but, well, it's still freaky to see her acting so weird."

"Sasha, we all want to be there for our friends, but the most important thing is that you're safe and you know what's best for you. You've got your dad, and your aunt Ginny and me, right?"

She nodded. "Dealing with Naomi can get so stressful."

"Being around Nip and Tuck helps, though, doesn't it?" Claire was never sure where today's reality for middle school students ended and Sasha's penchant for being a drama girl began.

"Of course. You're a good boy, aren't you, Nip?"

Sasha crooned to the cria as though she'd been raising llamas her whole life.

Steps crunched on the gravel drive outside the barn and Claire turned to see Dutch walking into the enclosure.

Sasha greeted him. "Hi, Dad! Why are you here so early?"

"Way to make a guy feel welcome. I thought I'd come and get you two and take you out to dinner."

Claire silently berated herself for the wobbly feeling in her stomach. "You don't need to take me to dinner, Dutch."

"Aw, come on, Claire. It'll be fun." Sasha eliminated Claire's wiggle room.

Dutch's enigmatic gaze was so bright Claire couldn't maintain eye contact. "Yeah, it'll be fun. You've done so much for Sasha, let us do this one thing for you."

Claire relented. He'd said *us,* not *I.* "Okay. But, Sasha, you still have a few chores to finish, don't you?"

"Oh, yeah." Sasha smiled, her braces glinting in the late-afternoon sunlight.

"Sasha, do you have your cell phone?"

"Yes. Right here." Sasha pulled the phone out of her front jeans pocket.

"Great. I'm going to talk to your dad outside for a few minutes until you're done, okay?"

"Sure."

Once she and Dutch were out of Sasha's curious earshot, Claire released a long breath.

"Is everything all right?" Dutch's tone was concerned without being accusative—which was an improvement.

She stopped near his truck and turned to him. "Dutch, what do you know about Sasha's friend Naomi?"

"Naomi?" His wrinkled brow betrayed his concern. "They were best buddies growing up, but I haven't seen Naomi around our house lately. Although she was at the sleepover." He frowned. "A very Goth-looking girl. Do you remember meeting her?"

"Yes. I'm asking because Sasha says Naomi is upset and shows signs of depression, or some kind of emotional distress." She rubbed her upper arms. "I'm not a psychologist or an expert with children, but you may want to call Naomi's parents."

"I'm not sure that would do any good." Dutch had one eyebrow raised, and his hands rested on his hips. "Do you think Sasha's hanging out with her too much?"

"Not at all. As a matter of fact, you can be proud of Sasha. She doesn't want to be part of Naomi's poor choices. But we may be talking about something Naomi doesn't have control over, like her mental health. Someone needs to know."

Dutch nodded. "I'll talk to Sasha, and I'll call the school in the morning." He paused. "You know Sasha can be a drama queen at times, don't you?"

Claire smiled. "We all can. But this is serious." She looked at him. "Be careful how you approach it with Sasha, Dutch. I don't want her to feel like I betrayed her trust. I just want her to be safe."

"Claire?" The sparkle was back in his blue eyes.

"Dutch?" She called on her emotional reserves to guard her heart.

"Thank you. You've come to mean a lot to both of us."

"Thanks, Dutch." She disregarded the comment about himself.

"Now, let's go to dinner." He smiled and her resolve melted in direct response to her attraction.

"Where are we going?"

"Nothing fancy—how about the diner?"

"Okay." Phew. The diner was busy and full of people. No opportunity to get too close to Dutch.

CLAIRE DIDN'T COUNT on her twin sisters being in the diner at the same time. Jewel and Jenna sat a large corner booth, talking.

"Hey, Claire!" Jenna waved them over. "Sit down and join us!"

Claire groaned. Dutch laughed.

"You sound like you don't love your sisters." His grin revealed that he understood exactly what she feared. No doubt he'd felt the same when they had dinner in Annapolis with his family.

"Claire, it's Jewel and Jenna!" Sasha squealed as only a preteen could.

The rare times Sasha had been at the farm when the twins stopped by they'd all gotten along famously. Claire hadn't minded, as she knew the twins were so much closer in age to Sasha than she was. Sasha could relate easily to Jenna and Jewel. They'd all grown up in the digital age. Claire still remembered the day cable television was hooked up in their living room. The twins hadn't been born yet.

Sasha skittered over to their booth. Claire saw Jenna slide quickly from her bench and into Jewel's, placing Sasha between them.

Great.

She and Dutch had a bench to themselves. The benches weren't that big and she knew that within a moment of sitting next to him her ability to focus would be gone.

Who was she kidding? It'd left when she'd gotten into Dutch's truck.

She followed Dutch to their booth. She didn't miss how the twins assessed Dutch from head to toe. Jenna was beyond obvious as she gave him a once-over, then raised her eyebrow as if to say, *So, I hear you like my sister.*

Jewel was more subtle. She sent him a quiet smile that said, *Either treat her right or get lost.*

"Good evening, Jenna, Jewel." He greeted them as though they met here regularly for family meals. Claire had to give him points for going along with their jocularity.

"Hi, Dutch. Taking the ladies out for dinner?" Jenna smiled, and Claire bit her tongue to keep from saying something rude.

"Actually, Sasha and I are taking Claire out. As a thank-you, this time without the boat."

The giggles that erupted from the twins and Sasha dissolved Claire's determination to play it cool. "Can't blame them," she said. "I wasn't much fun that day."

"Sure you were, Claire," Sasha insisted staunchly. If only that adoration would last. Chances were that, in a few years, Sasha wouldn't see Claire so uncritically.

Claire slid into the booth and Dutch got in beside her.

"Did you ever hear about the time Claire dated a midshipman at the Naval Academy?" Jenna went on to tell the awful tale of how Claire had puked all over one of the academy's sailboats. The mid was responsible for the condition of the craft when he returned it, so instead of taking her out for dinner he had to spend the evening bleaching it down.

Claire looked at the twins with what she hoped were shooting flames.

They made Sasha's matchmaking attempts appear amateurish—and Claire had been impressed with some of Sasha's manipulations over the past couple of months.

"When was this?" His lowered voice was solely for her ears. The twins and Sasha were gabbing away and didn't even notice that Dutch and Claire were having their own conversation.

"On one of my spring breaks." His expression made her laugh. "Dutch, it was a long time ago, and you were busy with your own life." In fact, it had happened after he and Natalie had become engaged.

He sighed and picked up his menu. She did the same, even though she knew what she wanted. From the diner, anyway.

"What did you two ladies order?" The timber of Dutch's voice and the heat of his thigh next to hers made Claire think of more than food.

"Dottie just took our order," Jenna said. "We like to come here on Fridays for the crab-cake platter."

"That's what I'm getting," he told her. "But I prefer the sandwich."

Dutch turned to Claire. She hadn't been in such close proximity to him other than the times they'd embraced. Heat crawled up her neck and she was sure her cheeks glowed.

Dutch laughed, a low and tantalizing sound. "Then crabs it is." He smiled at her and she wanted to grab a water glass and splash his face. They'd agreed to be cordial, friends. Not flirt in front of her twin sisters. He knew *exactly* what he was doing. Despite her attempt to keep everything on an even keel, she felt her mouth twitching.

"So, Dutch, Claire told us she's enjoying her time with Sasha, and that you all had a wonderful day in Annapolis." Jewel opened the conversation with that fairly neutral remark.

"Except for the seasickness." Jenna remained ever-practical.

Dutch turned back to the twins. Claire gave a silent sigh of relief at not being in his direct scrutiny for at least a moment. The pressure of his thigh against hers was enough intensity. She tried to scoot closer to the wall without being obvious, but Dutch pushed harder.

"Yes, she is, aren't you, Sash?" He reached over to pull Sasha's menu down and tweak her nose.

Sasha swiped him back. "Quit it, Dad!"

The whole table laughed. Claire loved hearing all their voices raised in such a joyful sound.

"Hey, Dutch." Dottie put down a glass of water in front of Dutch and nodded.

Dutch looked up. "Why are you working on Friday night, Dottie? I thought you'd stopped weekends."

Dottie blushed as if she'd been caught with the goods, but Claire wasn't sure what the "goods" were.

"Let me guess, Mel needs to come in later to get the baking done for Sunday's rush?"

At Dutch's teasing, Dottie swatted him on the head with her receipt book. "You mind your own beeswax, Dr. Archer. You tend to your animals and let me tend to my diner, okay?" Dutch laughed and Claire smiled. Dottie put her hand on her hip. "You've decided to dine with these fine gals, I take it? The usual?"

"You got it, Dottie." Dutch had dropped the subject of Mel. He understood that it was okay to tease Dottie a little, but he didn't want to embarrass her.

"You want the sandwich, right?"

"Yeah, not like these wimps eating them plain."

"Claire?" Dottie asked. "You want yours *plain?*"

Claire nodded, and Sasha said, "Me, too!"

As the twins laughed, Claire squirmed. She'd looked forward to a quiet night at home. Dutch's presence put a meal in practically the same league as a White House press event. She breathed deeply and tried to stay grounded. Tried to remember that she ran her own life.

Problem was, Dutch had been part of her life for so long, whether directly or indirectly. Even in D.C., the biggest reason she hadn't come back to see Natalie was her feelings for Dutch.

"Daddy?" Claire glanced over at Sasha. She usually called Dutch "Dad."

"Yes?" Dutch heard the different tone, too. Claire felt the slight tightening of his muscles. He knew he was being set up.

"When are you going to take Claire on a *real* date?"

The twins each grabbed their drinks and sucked them through their straws, eyes downcast. Sasha stared at Dutch. Claire watched Dutch as he stared back at his daughter.

Claire held her breath.

How was he going to get out of this one? She'd have to talk to her sisters about not encouraging Sasha—and staying out of her business. It seemed a bit precocious, even for Sasha, to ask such a question in public.

Dutch surprised them all.

"Next Friday night when you're on your school band trip."

CHAPTER SEVENTEEN

THE NEXT FRIDAY night, Claire opened the door to Dutch. He wore a sea-blue polo shirt and khakis, and his skin glowed from the sun. He presented her with a bouquet of peach-colored tulips.

"Thank you so much. You didn't have to do any of this, you know." She returned to the kitchen and checked the cupboard for a vase.

"I don't ever do anything I don't want to, Claire." He stepped into the kitchen and held his hand out to her. "Leave the flowers for now. They'll be fine. Let's go."

She placed her hand in his.

"You look beautiful." Dutch spoke as they walked out to the car.

"Thank you." She'd bought the pink spring dress especially for tonight. Casual but unmistakably feminine. It was sheath-style with a low-cut back, and the hem ended right above her knees. A lacy white cotton cardigan and strappy sandals made her feel elegant. Even sexy.

"Where's your truck?" She blinked at the dark convertible parked in her driveway.

"At home." He escorted her to the passenger door.

The wind caught his aftershave and its clean crisp scent tickled Claire's nose. Yummy.

"I didn't know you had another vehicle."

She slid into the black leather seat and he closed the door. "I keep it in the garage most of the time, especially in the winter," he said as he got in, then started the engine. "But I need it for nights like tonight." His eyes expressed the warmth of his mood.

Her awareness of him strung her nerves tight and they hadn't even left the driveway.

"How old is it?" She couldn't care less how old the car was. Whatever kept the conversation going—and away from more personal concerns—was fine with her. Anything to distract her from this close proximity to Dutch.

"I bought it for Natalie, but she never got around to driving it." He said it matter-of-factly, without sorrow or remorse. Claire took the opportunity to look at him as they drove onto the highway toward Baltimore.

"That's too bad. She would've loved it." Claire glanced around the plush interior. It was incongruous with the Dutch she knew. But tonight he was dressed up, and together she imagined they looked more like a city couple than a fiber farmer and large-animal veterinarian.

Shivers ran up her forearms, but not from the wind that blew around in the windshield. *She'd thought of them as a couple.* Until now she'd been so careful to keep them separate and apart in her mind. To her credit she'd never allowed her fantasies to inhabit a world where she and Dutch got along and were maybe even friends.

Or more.

"Are you warm enough?" Dutch had to shout over the wind and the noise of traffic. Even though the air was still crisp, the heated seats kept her comfortable.

"Absolutely! This is so much fun." Claire was grateful for the inconvenience of conversation at the moment. She needed mental space to get her thoughts in order.

And she needed to cool her body's reaction to Dutch or they wouldn't make it past the appetizers.

"Sit back and enjoy the ride," he shouted and grabbed her hand. He held it under his on the leather upholstery.

Claire's breathing sped up and she felt her heart quicken. This was going to ruin any attempts she made to distance herself emotionally from Dutch. The attraction that existed whether she acknowledged it or not. It simmered continually, and the tension kept her awareness of him constant. No matter where they were or what they talked about, it was there.

The silent promise that there could be something more between them if they could ever get past their emotional roadblocks.

She hoped she'd be able to enjoy the night and tried to pay attention to the evening sky.

They hit the Baltimore city limits and the water of the Inner Harbor spread out to their right.

The tension stretched Claire's nerves further than she'd realized they could be stretched. Dealing with her emotions over Natalie's life and death was hard enough for her. Trying to offer Sasha the support and love she craved added to the pressure, but time with Sasha gave her far more than she'd ever be able to give

Sasha. It was her desire for Dutch that pushed her to the edge of her self-control.

Claire leaned her head back and sank farther into the heated seat. As she observed the brilliant view of the Inner Harbor, she vowed to let it all go, if only for tonight. The sexual tension with Dutch might reach a bailing point. As long as she didn't forget that anything that happened between them would be just that—between them. And it wouldn't mean anything other than two people acting out of perfectly normal physical need.

DUTCH MANEUVERED the car through the city streets to a parking garage. He pulled into a spot on the roof and decided to take the elevator to street level. Claire's shoes didn't look as though they'd do well on metal stairs, and he liked the idea of being in an elevator with Claire.

Alone.

There'd be no going back if he took this too far, but he was tired of analyzing everything he did. The truth was that Claire had done a hell of a lot for him and Sasha. Especially for Sasha. He knew he was overprotective of his daughter, but he did know how to be a gentleman. He owed Claire a nice evening out, an adult thank-you. Even with their less-than-ideal past, he and Claire had been friends once. They could be again.

"Friends with benefits" is more like it.

He silently cursed himself for the thought and ushered her into the elevator. He put his hand on the small of her back and was thrilled to find that under her sweater her dress was open down to the base of her spine.

"Thanks." She went to move away, but as the door shut he pulled her to him.

"Claire." He rested his forehead on hers and was encouraged when she didn't draw back. "Let's put the knives away for tonight and just have a good time."

She didn't respond, but closed her eyes. He took the opportunity to touch her lips with his. She sighed against his mouth and he marveled at the softness of hers. He deepened the kiss.

The elevator dinged its arrival at the ground floor and the doors opened. Before Dutch could think straight enough to step back he heard a cough. He lifted his head and looked into Claire's laughing green eyes.

"Excuse us." He addressed the family that waited outside the elevator.

"You were kissing her!" A little boy he'd guess aged three or four pointed at him. The boy had a red balloon tied to his arm and it shook at Dutch.

"Yes, I was." Dutch glanced at the boy's parents, who didn't meet his gaze as they ushered their son onto the elevator.

"Way to be cool," he muttered in self-derision.

Claire grinned. "We'll never see them again. Besides, if that little boy hasn't seen his parents doing the same thing, then I'm sorry for all of them."

Dutch took Claire's hand and pulled her close to his side. The breeze had picked up, flattening her hair around her face. This was going to be a long dinner. Visions of all the things he wanted to do with Claire tormented him.

"What's wrong?" Lines appeared between Claire's brows.

"Wrong? Nothing." He took the leap. "Only that we're not alone right now."

He felt the shudder that ran up her arm.

She felt it, too. Their desire was mutual and strong.

He came to a halt near a retail building and eased her under the awning. The shoe store was closed as the nightlife began.

He continued to hold her with one hand and cupped her face with the other. She looked up at him, and he'd never seen such a beautiful expression of trust.

"Claire, you can tell me to stop right now."

She returned his gaze with a steady consideration that made him hard. Hell, everything about her made him hard.

"Let's do our best to enjoy our dinner, okay?" The huskiness in her voice stoked his fire as if she'd physically touched him.

He leaned in to kiss her and stopped himself. They were on one of the busiest streets in Baltimore, but it didn't matter. He wanted to push her up against the building and make love to her.

"Okay." He breathed in and straightened. Claire's face was neutral, but he didn't miss the shine of need in her eyes. She hadn't said no.

CLAIRE SIPPED her cabernet sauvignon. "Mmm." The wine's chocolate notes filled her palate. Its warmth was a perfect complement to the heat building from the nearness of Dutch.

"I'm glad you like it, but are you sure you don't want a glass of white to go with your rockfish?"

"No, no. This is lovely, thank you." She ran her finger

around the bottom of the crystal stem. "It's not supposed to matter anymore, is it? What wine you drink with what? As long as you like it."

"Hmm." Claire reveled in the solid lines of his face, made deeper and sexier by candlelight. How had the boy she'd grown up with turned into such a compellingly attractive man?

"What do you suppose Sasha's doing now?" The question left her mouth without any thought. Thinking about Sasha had become a big part of her day.

A smile tugged at his lips. "Why do you ask?"

"No reason. I hope she's having a good evening." Claire met his eyes and a laugh escaped her. "Okay. I do feel a bit guilty enjoying all of this without her."

"Why would you feel guilty? Sasha's twelve. Sure, she likes to come out with us and eat good food, but she'd be bored sitting here tonight."

And horrified that Dutch and Claire were throwing off sexual sparks like a transformer hit by lightning.

"She's on the school band trip, so I know she's safe and having a great time." Claire sipped her wine. "I wouldn't feel as comfortable if she was alone with Naomi."

"Naomi? Why on earth would you ever think I'd allow her to spend time alone with Naomi?" He'd told Claire after he'd spoken to Naomi's parents that, while he'd been discouraged by their blasé approach with their daughter, they'd assured him she was doing fine.

"Sasha's watching some of her childhood friends take different directions," Claire said carefully. "It's not easy. But she's sticking to her guns and hanging out with the well-balanced kids. You should be very proud, Dutch. Sasha has a good head on her shoulders."

"Yes, she does, and I have to thank you for helping her through these recent adolescent growing pains. She's grown so much in just a couple of months."

Claire leaned forward. She hated seeing him upset in any way over Sasha. He was such a good father.

"Dutch, don't worry about Naomi or any of Sasha's less-than-desirable classmates. She has a heart of gold, true, but she doesn't go looking for trouble."

"Hmm." He stared at his wine and Claire was entranced as the flicker of candlelight sparked blue stars in his eyes.

"Claire?"

"Yes?"

He reached across the table and held her hand.

"Let's not bring Sasha up again, okay? Tonight's for us."

Desire flamed inside her, and she smiled at him while wondering how she'd manage to eat her dinner when it was pretty clear what Dutch had planned for dessert.

Claire loved dessert.

THEY ATE SPRING leaf salad with mandarin orange sections and raspberry vinaigrette. Claire sampled Dutch's filet mignon and he tasted her broiled rockfish.

They talked. And talked some more. Claire did her best to catch Dutch up on everything she'd done in D.C. and during her first two years back in Dovetail. Dutch informed her of what he'd accomplished in vet school, afterward and in his business.

They didn't mention Sasha again. But they couldn't avoid Natalie.

Claire still felt guarded whenever Dutch talked to her about Natalie.

Tonight, though, his defenses were down. "I was so happy," he said. "*We* were so happy. When Sasha was born we often spoke of how blessed we were." She found his naked sincerity very moving.

"We were still so young, Claire. We'd finished college, got married and I still had vet school ahead of front of me. Yet we had a great income from Natalie's work as a state archivist, and it was all manageable." He sighed. "Until she got sick and it all went to hell."

He tapped his fingers on the table. "After the shock wore off, we were positive and hopeful. Her oncologist had several patients who'd beaten incredible odds and were in complete remission. But then the cancer came back a second and a third time." He rubbed his knuckles on the linen tablecloth.

Claire stayed silent.

"Natalie wasn't one of the lucky ones," he murmured.

"She *was* lucky, Dutch, in that she had you and Sasha. I know she didn't want to leave her life so early and would've done anything to stay here and raise her daughter. She never would've chosen to leave you. But your love and devotion gave her great comfort. And she knew you'd take care of Sasha."

Dutch looked up and Claire was shocked to see tears in his eyes. "I couldn't save her, Claire. I would've done anything. Anything." He broke eye contact and turned his head to the side. When he looked back at her, his eyes were brooding, dark.

"It was pure hell at times, but I never questioned it. Whatever it took to take care of Natalie was what I'd do. But I felt so much guilt that she was the one who got sick and not me. Sasha needed her mother more than a father and...it was all so unfair."

Claire didn't speak and he went on.

"She was sick for a very long time, Claire. The last three years we had no intimacy. All her strength went to fighting the cancer. I missed her, I missed us. And I don't want to sound selfish, but I missed our lovemaking."

Claire shook her head mutely.

"In the end it came down to assuring her that it was okay to go. That we'd all be okay. She'd suffered enough." Dutch looked at her. "Do you have any idea how hard it is to tell your wife that it's okay to die because she's suffered too much?"

"No, I don't," Claire whispered. The desire she'd felt had turned to waves of empathy for Dutch. Her guilt over her consuming attraction to Dutch hit bottom. How could she even *think* of being more than a friend to Dutch? How could she have thought of involving Sasha in what could never be a permanent relationship with her dad?

"No, of course you don't understand. How could you? Why would you?" Dutch grasped her hand. "I don't blame anyone anymore, Claire. There are no guarantees in this lifetime. Trust me, if there were, I would've cashed in on them long ago."

"Dutch, you and Sasha have been through a lot. You both have so much life still ahead of you. I really believe that for the two of you the best is yet to come."

She pulled her hand away and fiddled with her coffee spoon, embarrassed by the clichés she'd just spouted.

"Claire, I never meant to burden you with any of this." Dutch's voice was apologetic.

"You're not burdening me with anything, Dutch." She leaned back in her chair. "What you have done, though, is remind me why *this*—" she motioned between them "—is destined to remain a friendship. Period."

His eyes narrowed and he, too, leaned back in his chair.

"Oh?"

"Like I said, Sasha's been through so much. She deserves, and *you* deserve, a fresh start. No baggage from anyone's past." She gave him a smile then. It was the hardest smile she'd produced in a long while, maybe ever.

He seemed surprised for a moment. Then clouds of disappointment rolled in over his expression and put the more familiar frown on his face. "So that's it? End of story?"

Claire sighed. "Pretty much. It has to be this way, doesn't it, Dutch?"

He shrugged, didn't respond.

She splayed her fingers on the tabletop. "Of course, I'll be here for Sasha, and I won't let you stop her from seeing me. Not that you plan to. But I promised you when all of this started with Sasha that I'd put her first. Always. I meant it, Dutch."

This wasn't about *her.* Even if she and Dutch could contemplate a romantic relationship, their mutual history would prevent it from becoming permanent.

As she'd told him, Dutch deserved better. Sasha deserved better.

If Claire was going to live her newfound respect for the basics in life, she needed to take a fire hose to her lust for Dutch.

For Sasha's sake, if nothing else.

CLAIRE COULDN'T REMEMBER the ride back to Dovetail ever taking so long.

She studied his profile. His face was stern, which was evident even in the dark interior of the car. He'd kept the convertible top closed as raindrops had begun to fall on their walk from the restaurant to the car.

There wasn't any more conversation; they'd said all they needed to say. Her throat constricted and she knew she'd grieve the loss of the relationship they'd almost had, but she also knew they were doing what was best. Not just for Sasha, but for themselves.

It would only lead to constant disappointment if Dutch looked for Natalie every time he was with Claire....

She focused on the scene outside the passenger window as the trees sped by. When Dutch pulled into her driveway, she grabbed her purse and scarf. This was not going to be a prolonged goodbye.

He shifted the car into Park and Claire touched the door handle.

"Claire, wait." His voice was soft. Defeated?

She paused.

"This isn't the way we should end things. So…rough around the edges."

"Don't worry, Dutch, I won't let it affect Sasha or my time with her. And you and I don't have to talk except where Sasha or the llamas are concerned."

"This isn't about Sasha, Claire. Or the llamas."

"They're *all* it's about, Dutch." Tears threatened, and she didn't want to go through another heart-shredding dialogue with him.

Big splats of rain hit the windshield and the lightning they'd driven through lit up the sky around them.

"I'm going in before I get soaked. Thanks for dinner, and I'll see Sasha next week." Claire opened the door and hurried out into the wind and rain. She slammed the door shut and before she could change her mind made a fast break for the house.

CHAPTER EIGHTEEN

DUTCH LOOKED THROUGH his windshield and saw the stubborn lines of Claire's face, the determination in her stride. He listed every reason to let her go, to pull out of the driveway *now*.

A clap of thunder and simultaneous bolt of lightning were like electrical paddles to his heart.

You fool. You can't let her go. This is the time you two are supposed to have.

He pushed open his door and yelled as he stepped out. "Claire!"

He broke into a run as soon as his feet touched the dirt. In two, maybe three, more steps he'd reach her.

But she shortened the distance to nothing as she turned and ran toward him. They stared at each other. Wind-whipped leaves and rain pelted their faces, and the roar of thunder vibrated the air between them and the ground beneath their feet.

He was mesmerized by her. Standing still in the midst of the storm she looked like a goddess. She'd matured into a more beautiful woman than he could've imagined. Her wet hair blew about her face and her eyes shone with unshed tears. Tears his harsh words had caused.

"Claire, this *isn't* about Sasha. It's about you and me." He shouted over the roar of the storm. The rain became an all-out downpour, but he didn't care. All that mattered was that she understand him, that she see into his heart.

"I'll never be Natalie, Dutch," she shouted back, the effort of speech evident in the shivers that racked her shoulders and in the tautness of her neck. Her wet sweater was plastered against her pink dress and he saw the outline of her breasts, her nipples.

He reached for her, ran his hands up her neck and wove his fingers into her soaked hair. He lowered his mouth to her ear.

"It's Claire I want."

She stiffened with what he assumed was surprise. He didn't wait for her to soften her posture or release her stubborn pride. He moved his hands to cup her face and tilted her chin up with his thumbs. Her eyes were closed, her lips ready.

"Look at me, Claire."

She lifted her lids and he saw the battle that waged in the depths of her green eyes. The same battle that waged in his.

"Come with me, Claire. Let's go forward." He brought his lips to hers. First he licked them, then sucked at her bottom lip. Claire moaned and relaxed against him. She opened her mouth and the complete heat of his desire for her surged through him. There was no going back and he slid his hands down to her buttocks and brought her hips up against him.

He was home.

CLAIRE KISSED DUTCH with everything in her. He'd broken down every last defense and she was tired of fighting her desire for him. Their clothes grew wetter by the second in the downpour, and she had a vague thought that they should be more careful in the midst of a lightning storm. But thinking wasn't an option; she made a conscious decision to live in this very moment.

Dutch's hands were everywhere. He stroked the underside of her breasts and splayed his other hand across the bottom of her spine, his mouth firmly planted on hers. When she gasped with need he buried his mouth against her neck.

Her moan had nothing to do with fear of the storm around them, but with the intense storm of pleasure Dutch's lovemaking rained down upon her.

She wanted Dutch.

He wanted her.

"Claire," he groaned against her cheek as her hand found his erection. He pushed her back a fraction of an inch. "Let me make love to you."

She answered him by grabbing his hand and turning toward the house. They got up the steps, with her in front. When she fumbled with the key he used the opportunity to press up against her back and cup her breasts from behind. The raw elements raged in the storm around them, but the intensity of their desire seemed to create an invisible barrier from the elements.

Claire unlocked the door and turned the knob. They fell into the kitchen, and Claire wriggled out from under Dutch.

"We have to get out of these wet clothes," she whispered to his face. He was much closer than she'd realized in the dark.

"Damned right," he growled. He peeled off first his shirt, then his jeans. Claire's hands shook not with cold, but with want and need. The urgency of the moment, bordered on frightening, but fear was a small cost for the thrill of Dutch's caresses.

She got her sweater off and her dress down to her waist. She shrugged out of it. Dutch already stood in front of her, waiting, naked.

"Claire, why are you keeping your underwear on?"

She smiled in the dark kitchen. "Follow me."

They walked down the hall and into her bedroom.

Claire loved sex and loved being with a man who cared about her. But this was so much more. This was Dutch. They'd played in the sandbox and wading pool as kids and rolled in the sand at Ocean City as teenagers. He'd seen her naked more than once in their lifetimes.

Tonight he'd see her as the woman she'd become. And she was ready to accept him as that woman, to embrace the power of the chemistry that had always existed between them.

She'd raised her hands to remove her lingerie when Dutch reached across the gap and put his index finger in the side of her thong panties. He tugged and brought her closer to him as he caught the other side of the tiny garment and pulled down. As he did so he kissed her chin, her collarbone and then trailed his tongue down her abdomen.

His hands slid under her knees and he gently lifted

her legs, one at a time, out of the thong. She gasped as he left kisses on her thighs and headed back north. But he didn't bury his mouth between her legs. Instead, he stood back up and reached behind her. When he unhooked her bra and freed her breasts from their restraint, Claire felt a pang of need.

"Dutch, stop teasing me." She placed her hands on either side of his neck and pulled his mouth to hers.

"Oh, I'm not teasing you, baby."

He put his fingers on her lips whenever she tried to say anything.

It was time to stop talking.

Logic disengaged itself as Dutch's caresses grew firmer, bolder. When he slipped a hand between her legs and touched her with deft confidence, Claire's knees buckled. She drew him down on top of her as she fell to the mattress.

She stroked him. He groaned.

"Claire, I'm not going to last very long if you do that."

"Like this?" She continued running her hands over his erection and along his taut abdomen.

He replied with a bite to her neck. As soon as she moaned he kissed her nipple and sucked until she cried out. "Now, Dutch."

She stretched toward the nightstand to get a condom from the box she'd bought a few weeks ago—when she'd realized she could find herself in this situation with Dutch.

"I have a condom in my jeans."

"They're in the kitchen. Use this one."

She didn't think she could hang on to her sanity much longer. The kitchen seemed miles away. She wanted Dutch inside her. Here. Now.

Dutch positioned himself above her, an elbow on either side. He leaned down and kissed her with delicious thoroughness.

"Claire?"

"Now, Dutch."

He entered her, and the joining transcended their physical connection. Holding on to any sense of time or reality was impossible. Their hips moved with a need and longing that Claire had never imagined, let alone experienced.

It really was Dutch making love to her. Tears seeped out from under her closed eyes. As they both neared their climax, she made her last conscious decision of the evening.

Claire surrendered to her need for Dutch.

CLAIRE WOKE to the soft rustling of fabric. She opened her eyes in the pale morning light and remembered.

Dutch.

Making love.

She blinked and looked up.

His back was to her as he zipped his jeans. She glanced at her bedside clock. Only six.

"What's the rush?" Her voice sounded husky.

Sultry. Sated.

He turned back to face her in the semidark.

"I've got some patients to see this morning. Sasha

won't be back until late tonight and I have a lot to do at home."

His expression was inscrutable. Not because of the morning darkness, but because of the decidedly closed look he shot her.

Claire sat up and dragged the sheets with her. She held the bedclothes against her naked breasts. She found it odd that she felt so shy and vulnerable around the man she'd given everything to last night.

"Claire, I don't want to put us through this." He motioned with his hand, pointing briefly to her and then himself.

"Put us through *what,* Dutch? I thought the whole point of last night was that we'd buried our past."

And started something new. Hope snuffed out in her heart as quickly as her desire had flared.

His stance was too familiar. Angry. Stubborn.

"Claire, I should've kept this the way we knew it had to be. I'm sorry. This was a mistake. I'm not going to lead you on."

"And Sasha?" she said through numb lips.

"Sasha... Sasha will be fine. I'd never keep her from coming here. She's begun to think of you more as family than a friend. I can't take that away from her." His hand was on the doorknob.

He really was going to leave like this.

Claire tried to speak, but couldn't come up with any words. She'd be damned if she'd let him see her cry.

"Sasha will be back next week. I'll see you when I pick her up." With that he left. She heard the side door close behind him and flopped back onto her bed.

CLAIRE HEARD THE KNOCK at her back door through her sniffles. It had only been a few minutes, but she felt as though she'd been crying for the past decade. She supposed in some ways she had…

She wiped her cheeks with her sweatshirt sleeve and peered cautiously through her lace-curtained front window. She recognized the car.

The twins.

"Ugh." She wasn't in the mood for twenty questions.

They knocked again and she heard the murmur of voices as she went to the kitchen.

"Hey, come on in." Claire opened the door and immediately turned back toward the stove so they wouldn't see her face in the bright morning sunshine.

"We thought we'd come over and get your lists for the festival next weekend."

"Oh, uh, sure. Do you want some tea?" As soon as she asked Claire wanted to kick herself. Why was she inviting them to stay any longer than they had to?

"Claire, are you okay?" The caring in Jewel's voice hit Claire hard.

"No, actually, I'm not." She turned around and faced her younger siblings.

"What happened?" Jenna sounded shocked, as if she'd never thought her big sister could cry.

"Nothing. Everything. Well, nothing." Claire wiped her eyes, blew her nose into a paper napkin and looked directly at the twins.

"I'm finally letting go of some emotional baggage I've hung on to for way too long," she finally said.

The twins exchanged a worried glance.

"Come on, girls, I'm not losing my mind. In fact, I may have found *myself*."

The twins spoke in unison. "Huh?"

"What did you say?"

Claire breathed out her exasperation.

"I came home over two years ago to find out who I really am, and to belong to a community where I could become part of something special." She sniffled, but continued talking. "There's been unpleasantness at times, especially when I was confronted with the sins of my past."

"Give me a break, Claire. It's *us*, your sisters. We're not some cable news network." Jenna's stubborn streak was as wide as Claire's.

"You know you can trust us, Claire. You've always been there for us—let us be here for you." Jewel's green eyes were kind. Reassuring. Both girls were younger by more than a decade, but they weren't kids anymore. At some point they'd become women.

How had Claire missed that?

"This is obviously about Dutch." Jenna was matter-of-fact, no censure in her voice.

"Yeah, it is, but it's also about me, and Natalie and now Sasha." As soon as she said Sasha's name, Claire sank into the nearest kitchen chair and the tears fell again.

"I can't lose Sasha. I really love her as if she were my own. But Dutch and I— A future for us is too complicated, even if I wanted to try to change his mind."

Claire toyed with her napkin, remembering the scene this morning.

"I never thought he and I would ever be close again.

Or even pretend to be friends. But one thing's led to another, and with Sasha out here so often, I've...seen more of Dutch."

She grew silent. Mental pictures of Dutch in her barn, in her driveway, in this kitchen, in her bed—they all flashed through her mind.

"And?" Once again, the twins spoke in unison.

"Well, what do you think?" Claire rolled her eyes, sighed, then stared at her napkin. "Our attraction was always there, but lately it's been crazy—and last night, we, well, we made love."

"I knew it!" Jewel slapped her hands on the round table. Jenna hushed her.

"It has to be the stupidest thing I've done. Other than being there for Sasha, there's no room for me in Dutch's life."

"Claire, Dutch doesn't strike me as the type who'd get involved with any woman on a casual basis. He has his daughter to think about." That was Jenna, the practical one.

"But you two do have that old history—or was last night a type of closure?" Jewel was more the drama queen of the two.

"Closure?" Claire really hated seeing things in the light of day. It'd been a wonderful night with Dutch. If she was the romantic type she'd call it magical.

But facts were facts.

Dutch had been distant and withdrawn this morning. He hadn't even stayed for breakfast, and Sasha wasn't due to be picked up from the spring band trip until later tonight.

"You know, a way to put the past to bed." Jewel winced at her own pun.

Claire shook her head. "No, last night wasn't about closure, not for me." It'd been the natural result of the weeks they'd worked together in the barn, shared conversations about Sasha and, to some extent, the past. Last night, Claire had felt she and Dutch were alone for the first time. Without Sasha, obviously, but without Natalie's ghost, too.

"Why don't we get started on the Sheep and Wool Festival stuff and maybe as the day goes by you'll figure it out. I have a feeling that Dutch ran off scared. He'll come around, Claire."

"Yeah, maybe." Claire didn't agree, but had no energy left to argue with the twins.

She forced her mind on to the festival. She had a lot to accomplish and very little time to do it. She needed a plan.

"Let's get the pickup loaded by Wednesday night," she said, "so I can run it up to the fairgrounds Thursday. Since I may have to make two trips, I'd love it if one of you could ride up with me."

"I can." They spoke in unison yet again.

"Great. Let's get to the rest of the prep work." Claire threw herself into the tasks in a futile attempt to forget Dutch.

As if that was even possible.

CHAPTER NINETEEN

DUTCH STOOD at the kitchen sink and looked out at the bird feeders. He couldn't focus on any of the birds. Not the finches nor the pair of mourning doves that had made a nest in the clay house Ginny had hung with Sasha.

All he could see was Claire's milky skin under his hands. All he could hear were her murmurs. Their love-making had been damn near perfect, which made this morning that much harder.

This wasn't the first time he'd been with a woman since Natalie died, but it *was* the first time he hadn't compared her to Natalie. It had been Claire, no one else.

And it scared the hell out of him.

He'd moved on past Natalie's illness and death, as much as he could. But he had more than himself to think about. He had Sasha. And last night, in the middle of loving Claire, he'd forgotten about Sasha. He'd only been thinking of himself.

And Claire.

His cell phone rang and he looked at caller ID as it flashed on the counter.

Sasha.

"Hey, baby girl, what's going on?" He hoped he'd managed to keep his guilt—and apprehension—out of his voice. Sasha didn't usually call from a field trip.

"Dad, Mr. Flint wants you to phone him on his cell. He's pissed off because I was in the bathroom with Naomi too long and our group leader, Mrs. Sneller, couldn't find us."

He took a breath. At least Sasha was okay and unharmed.

"Hang on a minute, Sasha. First, cut out the bad language. Second, what do you mean you were in the bathroom? In your hotel room?"

"No, at the amusement park."

Dutch looked at his watch. "It's only ten o'clock. How long have you been at the park?"

"Since eight, Dad. They opened early for the schools, because we all performed yesterday." She didn't hide her annoyance.

"Watch the attitude, Sasha. I'm still not clear on why you were in the bathroom for so long."

She sighed impatiently.

"Naomi wanted me to come and talk to her. She's feeling all confused again."

"Confused? About what?"

"Ask Claire." Of course she knew about Naomi; she'd told him as much.

Before he could recall what Claire had told him, Sasha continued. "So I went in there to, like, talk to her and it took me an hour to convince her that she should, like, come back out and have fun on the rides with us. But by then we missed meeting everyone for the hourly check by the fountain, and Mrs. Sneller, like, freaked out and called Mr. Flint."

Dutch hated the cell phone sometimes. He'd much rather see Sasha in person so he could read her body language and have a better idea of what was truth and what was twelve-year-old histrionics.

"What's Mr. Flint's number?"

"It's on the permission slip that I left on the fridge."

He looked at the refrigerator door. "Got it. Stay close to Mrs. Sneller, okay? We'll talk more about this when you get home."

"Okay, okay."

Dutch pushed End and punched in Mr. Flint's cell number. He'd stayed calm through most of Sasha's girlhood dramas, but when she got her flippant attitude it infuriated him.

The call connected. "Mr. Flint."

Mr. Flint didn't elaborate except to say Sasha was a good kid, but her choice of a friend in Naomi wasn't in her best interests. As far as Mr. Flint knew, the girls hadn't been smoking or doing drugs, only talking as Sasha had said. Naomi was in the midst of a difficult home life. But the fact that neither girl had checked in with their chaperone for more than an hour was a violation of the field trip rules.

"Do you want me to come and get her?" Dutch checked the clock. He could be in Hershey, Pennsylvania, in about two hours.

"That won't be necessary. I think, in Sasha's case, having her call you and keeping her off the rides for the rest of the day will be enough." Mr. Flint had taught

Sasha since sixth grade; it'd been almost two years now. He obviously thought Sasha wasn't the problem, and Dutch believed him.

"I appreciate your talking to me, and for taking the time with Sasha. I'll address this further when she gets home."

"That's fine, Mr. Archer, but like I said, Sasha's not a bad kid. In fact, she's one of the good ones. I think she got herself too involved in whatever Naomi's problem of the day is and lost track of time."

"Okay, thanks." Dutch hung up, shaking his head. His daughter had told him to ask Claire about it. As if Claire knew more about raising a girl than he did.

Maybe she did.

He shook his head again. "What an idiot I can be, Rascal," he told the dog. Rascal looked up at him and whimpered as if he agreed.

WHEN SASHA GOT OFF the bus that evening, Dutch made a point of tracking down Mr. Flint and thanking him again. He sought out Naomi's parents and found her mother waiting, as upset as he'd been a few hours ago.

He herded Sasha into the truck and started home.

"I'm sorry, Dad. I messed up." He heard the genuine regret in her tone.

"I'm sorry, too, Sasha. It's not easy to say no to our friends, but when they choose the wrong path, we have to. If you're worried about Naomi, you tell me or a teacher at school. Tell the principal if you have to. But don't put yourself at risk for anyone, ever."

He drove the truck through the quiet streets of

Dovetail and let the silence settle a bit. Sasha needed to understand that he wasn't bending on this.

"Got it?"

"Yes, Dad." Her tired "you don't get it voice" was back. He'd take this up with her again in the morning. And maybe call Claire to ask if she'd talk to Sasha out at the farm this week.

Claire.

Why did he even kid himself that he could raise Sasha on his own?

CHAPTER TWENTY

CLAIRE COULDN'T BELIEVE her eyes. She'd participated in the Sheep and Wool Festival last year, but only as a volunteer. She didn't have enough fiber to sell yet, so she didn't think it was worth bringing any of her animals to show.

But this year exceeded all her expectations. Two of her llamas were in the barn, while the twin crias were in the adjacent stall. Sasha was looking after the twins while Claire went to get fresh-squeezed lemonade.

Thousands of festival attendees had the same idea and it took Claire more than thirty minutes to get through the concession stands.

Claire came back to the llama barn and her numbered stalls with two large lemonades. She scanned their surroundings. No Sasha.

She'd probably gone to the restroom. That was fine, but she should've called and told her if she couldn't wait for Claire to get back.

She put the drinks on a bench and pulled out her cell phone. She knew she was being overprotective, but didn't care. She couldn't shake a sense of unease. She needed to hear Sasha's voice to make sure all was well.

Sasha's phone rang and rang before it went to voice mail. Claire didn't leave a message, Sasha would see she'd called and text her back. That was what she usually did.

Claire watched the people streaming into the barn. They came in to get out of the spring heat and to look at the animals. Little kids never tired of seeing the llamas. Claire enjoyed talking to them, but not at the moment.

She had to find Sasha.

She walked into the stall to check on Nip and Tuck and to get a break from the crowds. She flipped open her cell phone and called Sasha again. A rattle in the corner of the stall caught her attention. It was coming from the bench where she and Sasha had left their water and personal items. Out of reach of the llamas and the public.

It was Sasha's cell phone, in vibrate mode. Claire grabbed Sasha's phone and stared at the caller ID in horror. She saw her own number.

Where was Sasha?

"How DID YOU EVEN get here, Naomi?" Sasha was perturbed as she walked with Naomi toward the woods outside the fairgrounds.

"I came in with my mom and her knitting friends." Naomi smirked. "She actually thinks I care about this stuff."

Sasha didn't like Naomi's tone, but besides being annoyed, she was afraid for her friend. If she could get Naomi to talk, she'd give the information to Claire so

Naomi would get the help she needed. Before she did anything stupid to herself.

"Why did you come with her if you don't like the Sheep and Wool Festival?"

"I told you, I figured you'd be here with your 4-H project and I wanted to talk to you." Naomi's sullen attitude was reflected in her flat tone.

"Well, I don't have much time. I'm here with Claire." Sasha liked pairing her name with Claire's. It made her feel safe, especially around Naomi when she was acting so weird.

Sasha went to finger her phone that she always kept in her front jeans pocket. Claire was a speed-dial away.

Sasha's stomach dropped when she found only a crumpled napkin. She'd forgotten her phone. If Claire or Dad tried to call her, they'd be worried. Worse, she'd get into trouble.

Naomi sighed and stopped midstride.

"What is it, Naomi?"

"Okay, I'll tell you, but don't freak out, okay?"

"Okay."

"Remember I told you I'm sad a lot and I can't snap out of it?"

"Yes." Sasha wondered if Naomi was going to tell her she was finally getting help from a doctor or someone.

"Well, I was hanging out with Melanie and her brother was there. He made us these amazing drinks— and guess what? I felt better afterward."

"What kind of drinks, Naomi?"

She felt sick again. She felt sick a lot when she was around Naomi.

"I told you not to get freaked out." Naomi shook her head. "It's no big deal. They have a little bit of vodka and something else in them, but they're so delicious and I feel great when I have them. I want you to try one and see for yourself."

"What? No way, Naomi! Are you crazy?"

"Hey, girls." A tall teenage boy walked up to them. He had a friend with him, also a teenager, but shorter and stockier. Sasha recognized him as her friend Maddie's older brother, Johnny. Unlike Maddie he was a terrible student and he'd been kicked out of high school. He had a bad reputation.

Fear took Sasha's breath away. She backed up.

"I gotta get back to the barn."

"What's the hurry?" Johnny reached out and, even though she'd moved away, he caught her with one arm. When she tried to slither out of his grasp, he wrapped both arms around her from behind. Sasha's breath came in quick gasps and she felt tears in her eyes.

Remember what Daddy taught you.

She took a deep breath and forced herself to relax. Johnny must have felt it and thought she was cool with everything. He slackened his grip a bit.

It was enough. Sasha scraped the heel of her cowboy boot down his shin as hard as she could.

"What the—!" Johnny's shin must have hurt. Out of the corner of her eye she saw the bigger kid start toward her. She twisted around and kicked Johnny in the crotch with all her might.

Sasha ran, but was tripped up by Naomi, who'd stuck her foot out. Sasha scrambled back up and glowered at her.

"You're *not* my friend!" She shocked herself with the strength and volume of her scream at Naomi.

She turned to run and saw that the two boys were still after her. She hadn't realized how far she'd walked with Naomi. They were on the fringe of the woods. She had a good quarter mile through dusty fields to get back to the festival.

She pounded over the sun-dried grasses. Thorns and twigs scraped at her legs, but she kept going.

Pretend it's gym class and you're being timed for the mile.

She heard the boys' footsteps behind her and ran harder, faster. When she saw the metal gates that cordoned off the festival, she felt a renewed sense of power. She was going to make it!

She got to the gate and climbed through. A security guard saw her and put his hand on her shoulder.

"Hold it right there, young lady."

Sasha couldn't catch her breath and bent over with her hands on her knees. She gasped out enough to let the guard know she wasn't trouble.

"They…they tried to…to drag me into the woods." She pointed over her shoulder. The boys and Naomi were mere dots as they ran the other way into the tree line.

"It's okay." The guard waited until Sasha caught her breath.

She straightened up and the guard saw her festival T-shirt.

"Where are you working at the festival?"

Sasha told him and gratefully walked back to the barn with the guard.

"HEY, HONEY." Dutch's deep baritone hummed in Claire's ear.

"Dutch, it's Claire, not Sasha. I'm using her phone. Oh, Dutch," Claire cried out. "She's gone and I don't know where she went. You have to come here now!"

"I'm in line for the parking lot. I'll be there in a minute."

Claire shut the phone and looked at the security guard she'd summoned. "That was her father. He's on his way. Have they made the announcement yet?"

"They're about to, ma'am." The guard spoke into her walkie-talkie for a moment, then turned back to Claire. "They're announcing it now. Don't worry, she's probably in line for funnel cakes or something. Kids do that every year."

"But it's not like her to leave her cell phone." Claire shivered with fear. "I'm going to go look for her again." She'd already run around the festival grounds, her eyes peeled for Sasha in her blue festival T-shirt. Her panic grew as each child she saw turned around and revealed that he or she wasn't Sasha.

"Ma'am, chances are your daughter's perfectly fine. But to be on the safe side, security's put up a perimeter and she won't get out, trust me. It's better for you to stay where you are. We don't want her coming back without you here, do we?"

Claire didn't correct the guard's assumption that she was Sasha's mother. Right now she felt the fear of a mother and it was a terrifying sensation.

Claire wrung her hands in spite of herself. A detached part of her knew that the security team was doing more than she could, but she couldn't separate her fear and anxiety from logical thought. She'd *die* if anything happened to Sasha.

"I'm sorry, I can't wait here." She turned from the guard to run out of the barn. She ran right into Dutch.

CLAIRE'S HEAD BUTTED against his chest and knocked his breath away.

Dutch grabbed her and held her at arm's length. "Tell me what happened."

Claire told him what she'd come back to after buying the lemonade. Her face was ashen and her eyes had a wild look he'd never seen before.

"And no one saw anything?"

"The couple in the other stall said they think she left with another girl." Claire's shaking hands pushed him away. "I've got to go find her, Dutch."

"No, Claire. *We'll* find her."

He looked at the security guard who'd walked up to them. "You the girl's father?"

"Yes."

"You'll be glad to know we've found your daughter. They're bringing her back here now."

Claire jumped up and hugged the guard. "Thank you so much!"

"No problem. Just doing my job."

CLAIRE TURNED to Dutch. His gaze was fixed on the barn entrance.

Sasha walked in with a guard and as soon as she saw Dutch ran over to him.

"Daddy!" She threw herself into his arms and Claire's tears spilled at their reunion.

He'd never forgive her for losing Sasha. Regardless of how happy the ending...

"Claire, I'm so sorry." Sasha let go of her dad and came over to hug Claire.

Claire hugged her and kissed the top of her dear, sweet head. Thank God she was okay. At least—

She straightened and lifted Sasha's chin with her hand. "You *are* okay, Sasha? Did anything happen to you?"

Sasha shook her head. "No, no—some loser friends of Naomi's tried to keep me with them and make me drink."

"Did you take anything?" Claire heard her pitch rise, but couldn't control it. "You didn't drink anything they gave you? What do you mean, they tried to *make* you drink? Did they lay a hand on you?"

The guard reappeared, accompanied by another one, an older man. "Ma'am, we have the other juveniles in custody and they'll be dealt with appropriately. Sasha already gave us her side of the story and, from the sound of it, she was very brave."

"Claire." Dutch's voice pierced through her haze of anxiety.

She looked into his blue eyes. Calm, wise blue eyes. Safety.

"Sasha's okay. We'll work it out." Claire blinked and glanced around. The two guards, several other farmers, Sasha and Dutch were all staring at her. As if *she* was the one who'd fought off an attack, who needed TLC.

"Ma'am, your daughter is safe. It's normal that as a mother you feel as though it happened to you."

Claire opened her mouth to correct the assumption that she was Sasha's mother, but no words came out.

The guard smiled at Dutch. "Dad, you've got two ladies to take care of tonight."

"Thanks so much." Dutch turned back toward Claire and Sasha. "Sasha, stay here with Claire. Security needs me to make a statement and sign a release." He walked out with the guards.

Sasha sat next to Claire on the small bench and laid her head on Claire's shoulder.

"You okay, kiddo?" Claire asked, stroking her hair.

"I'm fine. A little scared, but much better."

Claire hugged her tight as if she could will away the girl's pain. "Sasha, I'm so sorry I wasn't here when Naomi came by."

"She waited until you left. She knew I wouldn't go with her if you were here." Sasha looked back up at Claire.

"Why was I so stupid? Why did I believe her when she said she needed to talk to me?"

"Because she used to be your friend, Sasha. But she's a girl with serious problems. She's sick and needs help. It could happen to any of us." Claire stretched out her legs and kept her arm around Sasha.

They were both silent for a moment, then Claire said, "If I could somehow give you all the lessons I've learned in life, so you didn't have to suffer through learning them, I would. But that's not the way it is."

She continued to stroke Sasha's hair. "This won't be

the first time you'll be duped by a friend. You're a dear girl, Sasha, and you genuinely care about others. Sometimes you're going to attract people who are less than well. Try to remember what we discussed, about healthy boundaries."

"I guess I failed that lesson today."

Claire's heart heaved at the adult self-deprecation in Sasha's tone. "You didn't fail, Sasha. You're a survivor. You used what your dad taught you and got away from those jerks. You kept your head and you know what? You probably saved Naomi from a lot more trouble than she's already in."

Sasha nodded, then glanced up. "Dad's back!"

And he was, with bags of kettle corn and fresh drinks. "Ah, comfort food," Claire said with a smile.

CHAPTER TWENTY-ONE

CLAIRE HEARD the knock on the door as she walked from her bathroom into the kitchen, intent on making a cup of strong tea after her long shower. Sasha was safe, the festival was over and she'd fed the animals.

All of Monday stretched before her.

She wanted nothing more than to relax.

Her flash of fear at the prospect of a stranger at her door in the middle of the morning was replaced by relief when she saw Dutch's profile through the window's lace sheers.

She made sure her terry robe was belted tight and opened the door.

"Dutch—is everything okay?"

He seemed on edge. "Yes. Can I come in?"

"Of course." She gestured him inside.

His presence immediately filled the room. She tried to keep her eyes off his arms, his legs. Dutch had always loved to run and obviously still did. The workout T-shirt and running shorts showed off his toned body. Leaner and stronger than he'd been as a teen or young man, he exuded a sexiness that made Claire's knees feel like mud.

The warm spring air drifted into the kitchen. Claire

caught the scent of the apple blossoms from her small orchard.

Dutch stared at her. She squirmed under his scrutiny. Was he angry, sad, upset with Sasha again? Had he decided it was Claire's fault that she'd been left alone long enough to be tempted away by Naomi?

"What?"

"Do you have any idea what you did at the festival?"

"Put Sasha at risk?"

He shook his head with impatience. "No, *no,* Claire. It wasn't your fault. But how you reacted to it—" he paused, studying her "—it was as though your own child had disappeared."

Claire's throat constricted and she was unable to find any words.

Dutch moved in close, too close. His eyelashes framed his eyes with their blue irises and emphasized how dilated his pupils were.

With need. Desire.

"It was as though you're Sasha's mom," he repeated.

She looked up at him, eyes wide. He stared at her with a purpose that made her toes wriggle against the hardwood floor.

"You're beautiful."

"But I should've— Sasha could have…" She couldn't verbalize her deepest fear.

"You were thinking on your feet. Called security. And Sasha knew to get out of there when she smelled trouble."

"Only because you taught her self-defense."

"No." He leaned toward her. She thought he'd kiss her. Prayed he would.

"Claire, *we* taught her how to handle the whole situation. We prepared her together. Supported her 4-H project. Let her be herself, even when she tried to matchmake us. Ever since you came into her life, we've taken care of her, raised her—as a team."

He reached for her and she went into his arms.

His hands tugged her hair free of the band she held it back with. His stomach was pressed against her, and she felt the hair of his legs against her smooth shins.

His eyes were dark and heavy-lidded and he looked at her one last time, gave her a chance to back out.

"I'm tired of trying to think my way out of this, Claire. I want you."

"I want you, too, I—" Before she'd finished, his mouth was on hers, moving with passion and familiarity as if they were a couple who'd been apart for years, finally reunited.

But this wasn't a reunion or a homecoming. It was a joining—all heat, need, sweat and intensity.

Time was nonexistent, yet Claire knew it couldn't have been more than forty seconds before Dutch had her sash untied and her robe in a pool around her feet. He grabbed her and pulled her against his arousal. Claire moaned.

"Dutch, I—"

"Shh. We've talked enough for three lifetimes, Claire. Let me make love to you."

She pulled back a fraction of an inch. "There won't be any regrets this time?" She whispered her fear aloud.

"Only if you don't kiss me."

She lost her train of thought as he trailed kisses on the nape of her neck, then bit the curve of her shoulder.

"God, Claire, you're so beautiful." He stared openly at her breasts, her stomach, her legs. His gaze met hers. "I've been such a fool. Can you forgive me?"

"Forgive you?"

"I almost blew this for both of us. For all of us."

"Then *we* need to make up for it."

"DAD?"

"Hmm?"

They sat at the dining-room table. Sasha's math book was open, but Dutch hadn't seen her writing anything for the past fifteen minutes. He couldn't focus on his case studies, either.

"I miss Claire when she's not here. Or when we're not at her house."

Sasha's face looked so somber. She'd grown up over the past year, but not as much as she had in the past few weeks. The incident at the Sheep and Wool Festival had shaken her, and after the shock had worn off, she'd needed a lot of comfort.

He gave her all the comfort he could, but in his heart he knew where she'd healed the most.

In Claire's arms. Through her hugs, and kisses and their long talks as they sat together on the couch.

"I know, pumpkin. She makes a difference to everyone she meets."

"What about you, Dad?"

Her eyes were round and innocent, but he recognized the determination in their depths. That same determination was what had kept Natalie alive far beyond the medical prognosis. It was what had allowed Claire to stand her ground with him for Sasha's sake.

"I miss her, too."

"Do you want her around all the time?" she asked.

"Sasha, she *is* around all the time."

"You know what I mean, Dad." Sasha tapped her eraser on the open book.

"I've been thinking, Dad. I'm tired of calling her Claire. I don't want to call her Aunt Claire, either."

"So? What *do* you want to call her?" He held his breath. Both their lives hinged on her reply.

"I want to call her Mom."

She put her hands down on the table, a young girl verging on womanhood. "Dad, I'm not trying to replace Mom. In my heart I feel Mom loves Claire and brought her to me. I want to call her *Mom* because that's what she is to me now."

Dutch had to wait a moment to speak. Even so, tears burned his eyes and his vision blurred.

"You're a lucky girl to have had two wonderful women in your life to call Mom."

"Aw, Dad, I'm sorry. I don't want to make you sad."

"I'm not sad, sweetheart. I'm so proud of you I could burst. And I'll let you in on something I suspect you're already aware of."

"What?"

"There's one other name I'd like Claire to have. Ours. Archer."

With a whoop, Sasha scrambled over to Dutch for a hug. All they needed to complete their circle was Claire.

CHAPTER TWENTY-TWO

THREE BUSY WEEKS after the drama at the Sheep and Wool Festival, Claire sat in front of her vanity mirror and put on her makeup. She hoped that she'd be able to keep her cool through the next few hours. The shop was finally ready for the opening gala. She'd sent out invitations with one of the photos Sasha had taken of Nip and Tuck as a backdrop. The knitting group had pledged to come, along with all their friends and family. Her parents were coming.

Dutch and Sasha would be there; so would Dutch's parents and Ginny.

Although they'd grown even closer ever since the festival, she'd been careful not to question the exact status of their relationship. She didn't want Dutch to feel any pressure from her for something more permanent. She promised herself that she'd be grateful for their relationship as it was.

She smiled as she realized she couldn't wait for him and Sasha to get here.

The twins had already arrived and were making her crazy.

"Don't you want to wear a dressier outfit? This is a

celebration!" Jewel turned up her nose at Claire's white capri pants and simple mint-green blouse.

"Yes, it's a celebration—in a cottage yarn shop, for heaven's sake. And it's a crab feast, not a candlelight dinner." Claire silently cursed her shaking hand as she messed up her eyeliner for the second time.

"Here, let me get that for you. Sit on the bed." Jenna stepped in and finished Claire's makeup.

"I don't look like a clown, do I?"

"No. You look absolutely beautiful, like a woman who's about to start a new life for herself." Jenna admired her own work.

"I did that almost three years ago."

"But you've really changed these last six months. And now you're opening up the yarn shop. You've been talking about it since you came back to Dovetail."

Jewel stepped closer and studied Claire critically. "Good job, sis!" she said approvingly, then high-fived Jenna.

"Are you going to tell us the name of the shop yet?" Jenna asked.

"You guys didn't look under the cover, did you?" Claire had gone to great pains to cloak the shop's sign with a huge length of burlap. She'd pull it down tonight when all her guests were there.

"No, but how have you managed to keep it quiet for so long?"

"What about business cards, flyers, advertising?"

As the twins fired questions at her, she glanced at her alarm clock. Two hours and thirty-three minutes until the party.

"It wasn't that difficult," she replied. "I've had everything made up, but haven't put any of it out yet. You saw the invitations—it said, *the cottage shop at Llama Fiber Haven.*"

"We don't even get a hint?"

"We've helped you with so much of this!"

Claire held up her hands as if warding off vampires.

"No, I'm not telling. You'll have to wait like everyone else."

THE NIGHT WAS SULTRY, but with enough of a breeze to make it bearable. Claire had the air-conditioning on in the shop, but since her guests would enjoy a catered dinner under a tent adjacent to the cottage, she was grateful for the break in heat.

She'd lighted votives in lanterns shaped like sheep; they illuminated the path from the drive, where people could park, to the tent and shop.

Crabs steamed in the caterer's huge pots, and long picnic tables were covered with brown butcher paper. Claire's invitations had said it was going to be a big crab feast, Maryland-style.

Claire made sure the coolers were full of water, sodas and beer. Wine chilled in tubs of ice on the serving tables.

All the physical details were complete. Claire looked up at the cottage, where she saw her parents and sisters standing together outside the shop, laughing. Claire loved her family. With a pang she acknowledged that she wanted one of her own someday.

Enjoy tonight for what it is. You have so much to be grateful for.

She knew this, but still couldn't keep visions of Dutch and Sasha out of her mind. Dutch's lovemaking was ardent and it was so easy to believe he had the same thoughts as she did about their future.

But he never talked about it. They never spoke of the past anymore, either. That was good. But was their future destined to remain unaddressed, as well?

CLAIRE CAME to the end of her brief welcoming speech. "Thank you all for coming. Now, there's one more thing I want to do before we all pig out!" Claire smiled at her guests. There were more than seventy-five people, but she was most aware of one.

Dutch.

He watched her as he stood behind Sasha. They'd come to the cottage with the last group of arrivals.

Claire's hands were sweating and her mouth was paper-dry. She reached up to pull on the makeshift hemp cord she'd attached to the store's sign. The sign hung over the door and she had to walk to the side to get the burlap to slip off easily.

As the rustic fabric dropped to the ground, Claire smiled at her shop's sign.

Natalie's.

Some of the guests murmured, some let out soft gasps. Claire didn't care about anyone's reaction except Sasha's and Dutch's.

Sasha jumped up and down and clapped in appreciation. Tears started in Claire's eyes. Her gaze landed on Dutch and, although he didn't smile, his eyes sparkled and he was clapping, too. Was he holding back tears?

Claire stepped off the porch and walked over to Dutch and Sasha. "Is it okay with you?" She looked at Sasha, who hugged her in response.

"I love you, Claire." Sasha's voice was muffled by Claire's shoulder. "Of course it's okay."

"I love you, too, kiddo."

Claire looked up at Dutch.

"And you?" She needed to know he approved of the name.

"I love you, too, Claire." Shock jolted through her and her expression must have shown her surprise as Dutch laughed aloud.

"Come here." He embraced her in a hug that included all three of them.

"WAIT, DAD!" Sasha wriggled out from between Dutch and Claire as they sat on the couch in Claire's living room. The guests were gone, the caterers had packed up. The three of them were curled up, relaxing after the evening's events.

Sasha ran to the kitchen and came back carrying two huge shopping bags.

"First, this is for you, Dad. Claire and I did it." Claire held her breath as Dutch took the bag, delighted by his startled expression.

"This is Claire's night, Sasha."

"It's *all* of our nights, Dad. Just open it."

Dutch pulled out the sweater and his hands stilled. "The sweater." His voice was a whisper.

"I asked Claire to help me finish it and we did it, just like Mom would have wanted."

"We owe Mr. Black some credit here, too," Claire added. Dutch was so quiet—was he upset?

He reached out his hands to Sasha and drew her close. "Come here." She went to her dad, smiling.

Dutch looked up at Claire. "Claire, you realize we're all in this together now, don't you?"

"I never had any doubt, Dutch."

Sasha pulled away from her dad. "Now it's Claire's turn." They nodded at each other and Dutch sat up. "This is for you, Claire."

"What on earth?"

Dutch pulled a huge bouquet of red roses from the bag and gave them to Claire. She turned to him, then Sasha, then back to Dutch.

"Thank you so much. You shouldn't have."

"Wait a minute. We're not done." Sasha pulled out another bouquet, pink roses this time, and handed them to Claire. "These are from me."

Claire laughed. "Okay, but you both didn't—"

"We're not done!" They spoke in unison, which made Claire laugh more.

Dutch removed a small box from his pocket.

A ring box.

Both Dutch and Sasha got down on their knees in front of the couch.

"Will you marry me?"

"Will you let me call you Mom?"

Tears streamed down Claire's face. "You don't have to do this. The shop will always be Natalie's. It's where Sasha and I spent so much time. The knitting and llamas and yarn tie us all together."

"Claire, we planned this before we knew what the name of the store was going to be." Dutch was still on his knees. "Answer me, Claire."

Sasha stayed on her knees, too, and smiled at Claire. She knew the answer.

"Yes. Yes!" It was the easiest reply Claire had ever given. It came from her heart.

Sasha leaped up and hugged her so tightly that Claire toppled over and landed on her back. The two bouquets of roses spilled onto the coffee table.

Sasha jumped up. "Claire, I'm so sorry!" But she kept laughing.

Dutch's face appeared in Claire's vision before she had a chance to sit up.

"Right where I like you," he whispered. He kissed her long and hard.

Dutch stood and helped Claire get back on her feet. He pulled her into his arms.

"I'm in love with you, Claire, and I want to be your husband. Will you have me?"

"I told you, Dutch, I'm not going anywhere."

* * * * *

HARLEQUIN *Super Romance*

COMING NEXT MONTH

Available June 29, 2010

#1644 CHARLOTTE'S HOMECOMING
The Russell Twins
Janice Kay Johnson

#1645 THE FAMILY PLAN
Suddenly a Parent
Susan Gable

#1646 PLAYING WITH FIRE
The Texas Firefighters
Amy Knupp

#1647 ONCE AND FOR ALL
Single Father
Jeannie Watt

#1648 THE COWBOY SOLDIER
Home on the Ranch
Roz Denny Fox

**#1649 BEGINNING WITH
THEIR BABY**
9 Months Later
Tracy Wolff

LARGER-PRINT BOOKS!
GET 2 FREE LARGER-PRINT NOVELS PLUS
2 FREE GIFTS!

◆ HARLEQUIN®

Super Romance

Exciting, emotional, unexpected!

YES! Please send me 2 FREE LARGER-PRINT Harlequin® Superromance® novels and my 2 FREE gifts (gifts are worth about $10). After receiving them, if I don't wish to receive any more books, I can return the shipping statement marked "cancel." If I don't cancel, I will receive 6 brand-new novels every month and be billed just $5.44 per book in the U.S. or $5.99 per book in Canada. That's a saving of at least 13% off the cover price! It's quite a bargain! Shipping and handling is just 50¢ per book.* I understand that accepting the 2 free books and gifts places me under no obligation to buy anything. I can always return a shipment and cancel at any time. Even if I never buy another book from Harlequin, the two free books and gifts are mine to keep forever.

139/339 HDN E5PS

Name _____ (PLEASE PRINT)

Address _____ Apt. #

City _____ State/Prov. _____ Zip/Postal Code

Signature (if under 18, a parent or guardian must sign)

Mail to the **Harlequin Reader Service:**
IN U.S.A.: P.O. Box 1867, Buffalo, NY 14240-1867
IN CANADA: P.O. Box 609, Fort Erie, Ontario L2A 5X3

Not valid for current subscribers to Harlequin Superromance Larger-Print books.

**Are you a current subscriber to Harlequin Superromance books and want to receive the larger-print edition?
Call 1-800-873-8635 today!**

* Terms and prices subject to change without notice. Prices do not include applicable taxes. N.Y. residents add applicable sales tax. Canadian residents will be charged applicable provincial taxes and GST. Offer not valid in Quebec. This offer is limited to one order per household. All orders subject to approval. Credit or debit balances in a customer's account(s) may be offset by any other outstanding balance owed by or to the customer. Please allow 4 to 6 weeks for delivery. Offer available while quantities last.

Your Privacy: Harlequin Books is committed to protecting your privacy. Our Privacy Policy is available online at www.eHarlequin.com or upon request from the Reader Service. From time to time we make our lists of customers available to reputable third parties who may have a product or service of interest to you. If you would prefer we not share your name and address, please check here. ☐

Help us get it right—We strive for accurate, respectful and relevant communications. To clarify or modify your communication preferences, visit us at www.ReaderService.com/consumerschoice.

HSRLP10R

HARLEQUIN®

A Romance

FOR EVERY MOOD™

Spotlight on
— Heart & Home —

Heartwarming romances
where love can happen
right when you least expect it.

See the next page to enjoy a sneak peek
from Silhouette Special Edition®,
a Heart and Home series.

CATHHSSE10

Introducing McFARLANE'S PERFECT BRIDE
by USA TODAY *bestselling author Christine Rimmer,*
from Silhouette Special Edition®.

Entranced. Captivated. Enchanted.

Connor sat across the table from Tori Jones and couldn't help thinking that those words exactly described what effect the small-town schoolteacher had on him. He might as well stop trying to tell himself he wasn't interested. He was powerfully drawn to her.

Clearly, he should have dated more when he was younger.

There had been a couple of other women since Jennifer had walked out on him. But he had never been entranced. Or captivated. Or enchanted.

Until now.

He wanted her—*her*, Tori Jones, in particular. Not just someone suitably attractive and well-bred, as Jennifer had been. Not just someone sophisticated, sexually exciting and discreet, which pretty much described the two women he'd dated after his marriage crashed and burned.

It came to him that he...he *liked* this woman. And that was new to him. He liked her quick wit, her wisdom and her big heart. He liked the passion in her voice when she talked about things she believed in.

He liked *her*. And suddenly it mattered all out of proportion that she might like him, too.

Was he losing it? He couldn't help but wonder. Was he cracking under the strain—of the soured economy, the McFarlane House setbacks, his divorce, the scary changes in his son? Of the changes he'd decided he needed to make in his life and himself?

Strangely, right then, on his first date with Tori Jones, he didn't care if he just might be going over the edge. He was having a great time—having *fun,* of all things—and he didn't want it to end.

Is Connor finally able to admit his feelings to Tori,
and are they reciprocated?
Find out in McFARLANE'S PERFECT BRIDE
by USA TODAY bestselling author Christine Rimmer.
Available July 2010,
only from Silhouette Special Edition®.

Copyright © 2010 by Christine Reynolds

SSEEXP0710

Love Inspired

Bestselling author

JILLIAN HART

launches a brand-new continuity

ALASKAN *Bride* RUSH

*Women are flocking to the land of the Midnight Sun
with marriage on their minds.*

A tiny town full of churchgoing, marriage-minded men? For
Karenna Digby Treasure Creek sounds like a dream come true.
Until she's stranded at the ranch of search-and-rescue guide
Gage Parker, who is *not* looking for love. But can she *guide* her
Klondike hero on the greatest adventure of all—love?

KLONDIKE HERO

*Available in July
wherever books are sold.*

Steeple
Hill®

LI87608

www.SteepleHill.com

HARLEQUIN®

INTRIGUE

BESTSELLING
HARLEQUIN INTRIGUE AUTHOR
DEBRA WEBB
INTRODUCES THE LATEST
COLBY AGENCY SPIN-OFF

COLBY AGENCY

MERGER

No one or nothing would stand in the way
of an Equalizer agent…but every Colby agent
is a force to be reckoned with.

Look for
COLBY CONTROL—*July*
COLBY VELOCITY—*August*

www.eHarlequin.com

HI69483

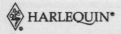
HARLEQUIN®

Showcase

LESLIE KELLY
Naturally Naughty

Wicked & Willing

On sale June 8

Reader favorites from the most talented voices in romance

Save $1.00 on the purchase of 1 or more Harlequin® Showcase books.

SAVE $1.00 on the purchase of 1 or more Harlequin® Showcase books.

Coupon expires November 30, 2010. Redeemable at participating retail outlets.
Limit one coupon per customer. Valid in the U.S.A. and Canada only.

52609057

Canadian Retailers: Harlequin Enterprises Limited will pay the face value of this coupon plus 10.25¢ if submitted by customer for this product only. Any other use constitutes fraud. Coupon is nonassignable. Void if taxed, prohibited or restricted by law. Consumer must pay any government taxes. Void if copied. Nielsen Clearing House ("NCH") customers submit coupons and proof of sales to Harlequin Enterprises Limited, P.O. Box 3000, Saint John, NB E2L 4L3, Canada. Non-NCH retailer—for reimbursement submit coupons and proof of sales directly to Harlequin Enterprises Limited, Retail Marketing Department, 225 Duncan Mill Rd., Don Mills, ON M3B 3K9, Canada.

U.S. Retailers: Harlequin Enterprises Limited will pay the face value of this coupon plus 8¢ if submitted by customer for this product only. Any other use constitutes fraud. Coupon is nonassignable. Void if taxed, prohibited or restricted by law. Consumer must pay any government taxes. Void if copied. For reimbursement submit coupons and proof of sales directly to Harlequin Enterprises Limited, P.O. Box 880478, El Paso, TX 88588-0478, U.S.A. Cash value 1/100 cents.

5 65373 00076 2   (8100)0 11654

® and TM are trademarks owned and used by the trademark owner and/or its licensee.
© 2010 Harlequin Enterprises Limited

HSCCOUP0610